Brotherhood:

Stories by The Wilson Boys

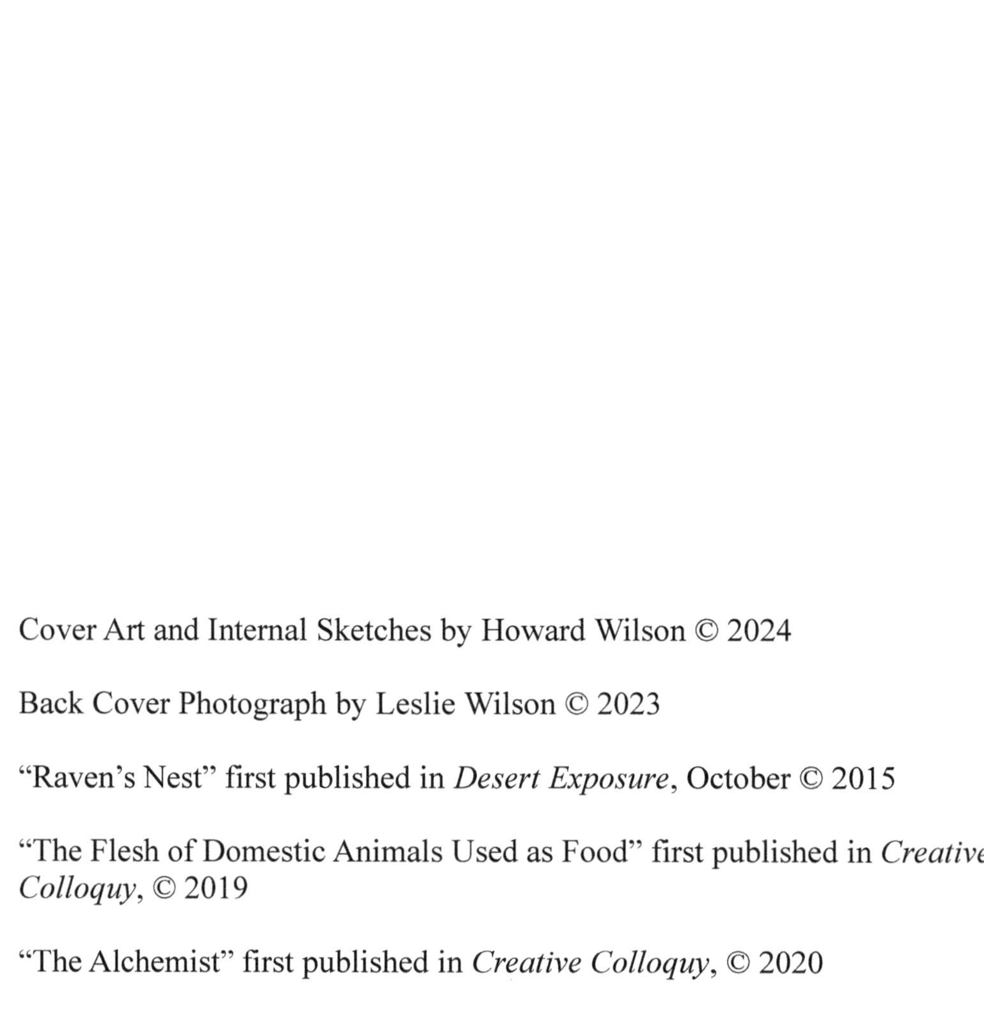

Table Of Contents

Introduction

O ur family is one of readers. Our parents read, it seemed, constantly. So, we children—four boys and two girls—read. In fact, we read everything, anything: cereal boxes, toothpaste cartons, encyclopedias, newspapers, mom's magazines, dad's magazines, comic books, school books…anything. Another part of our heritage was story-telling. Our father told us stories of his childhood, and we loved them; we wanted to hear them again and again. But reading stories and hearing them wasn't nearly enough for our starving minds. We made up stories and turned them into plays which we produced in our garage, hoping to add a few cents to our meager allowances.

As we grew up, married, and had our own children, we added our own tales to those of our parents; our children loved (?) them all. We also began writing, not just business letters, but stories. When Chas was in Turkey, he and Bruce traded first lines of stories that required the "receiver" to write a 1,000-word short story without changing the provided opening sentence. (Some of those are included in this anthology.) Howard joined us later in this effort. Within the past decade, we three brothers have written many more stories, shared them with one another, and eventually saw some of them published in literary journals and monthly news publications. At some point along this literary journey, one of us (or maybe all of us) wondered if we could produce an anthology, a collection of *our* favorite, *our* best efforts at short fiction. What you hold in your hands is our offering—fifteen stories written by three brothers over a long period of time.

Although our brother, Joel, passed away more than fifty years ago, he was also a writer. In his honor, we have included three poems he wrote, which were published in a literary journal while he was in college.

We Wilson Boys, The Brotherhood, hope you enjoy the variety of fiction that was fed by our life of reading, nurtured by the stories we heard, and allowed to spill forth from our minds onto the enclosed pages.

Raven's Nest
by Bruce Wilson

A year after Sarah's death, Alex knew it was time to go through her closet, even though he was unable to forget the dreams that urged him to open it and face his fears.

~~~

On the day of her funeral, Sarah's children had chosen a few keepsakes without ever going into the closet, and he'd never heard from them again. Perhaps he should have been upset with them; after all, he'd nursed their mother through two terrible years of chemo, watched as her crystal blue eyes dulled, and even held her in his arms as she passed into whatever came after life. But Alex wasn't bothered by their lack of interest
~~~

in him. He wasn't their father and hadn't met them until they were young adults. They'd always treated him cordially, but he thought that was because Sarah would've been upset with them if they'd done otherwise. Still, a simple gesture, a call or a visit, would have been nice.

The past year had been rough for Alex. He'd thought about seeing a counselor a few times, but he'd never made an appointment. During that time, he'd learned how to get through the sad and lonely days without crying; still, he spent a lot of time trying to figure out why some days were better than others. Mornings had been really hard on him since he and Sarah had enjoyed starting their days together. He'd finally created a new routine and it had seemed to work.

~~~

After Alex woke up, he headed to the kitchen and made himself a cup of coffee and a piece of toast. Then he put on his old flannel robe, grabbed the morning paper off the porch, and went out into the back yard. He sat at the patio table and watched the birds flurrying around the feeders hanging in the junipers. The sun hadn't yet peeked over the fence, but the bottoms of the few clouds in the sky were changing from light gray to orange. Alex had just lifted his cup in a salute to nature when a chill climbed up his spine and raised the hair on the back of his neck. He shivered and pulled the collar of his robe tighter. The cool morning air seldom bothered him; icy mornings growing up in Minnesota had given him immunity to the gentle breezes of the Southwest. Yet the raw cold had been real, reminding him a little too much of the Iron Range.

He pulled the rubber band off the rolled-up newspaper and spent a moment trying to flatten out the wrinkles. The ritual was necessary for a daily paper that managed to reach eight pages on a good day. The headlines were usually about local politics, and the back page was dedicated to the high school sports teams. He turned to the inside, searching for the crossword and Sudoku puzzles. Reaching into the pocket of his robe, Alex took out the ballpoint pen he kept there, clicked it open, leaned over the table and started filling in the puzzle.

A delicate voice uttered, "Alex."

He dropped the pen and turned around, first one way and then the other. *That's odd*, he thought, as he stood and walked into the house, shaking
~~~

his head, wondering if he'd left the radio on. Alex ended up in the bedroom and stood at the foot of the bed for a moment.

"What the hell was that?" He said out loud, his words filling the quietness. Then he laughed at himself, the nervous chuckle a self-confirmation that he probably was going crazy. He stared at the jumbled covers on the bed and wondered if he was getting old or just imagining he'd heard his name.

Alex went back outside and sat at the table. He took a sip of the lukewarm coffee and picked up the pen. He glanced at the first clue on the crossword and read aloud, "One across, 'a mental image of something threatening.'" He couldn't come up with the seven-letter word, but he knew the feeling, so he moved on to the next clue and the next. By the time he finished the crossword, the Sudoku, and his coffee, the back yard was filled with the morning sun. The small birds had flown off, and Alex could hear the odd clucking sound of the ravens tapping their bills on the tree limbs and picking at the purple berries in the trees.

One of the large black birds soared into the yard and lit on the small concrete birdbath near the adobe wall. Alex was surprised; he'd never seen a raven so close, let alone watched one drink from the birdbath. It seemed to glare at him with its black eyes. He glanced down at the small chunk of toast he'd left on his plate and tossed it at the raven to see if it would leave. But the bird didn't move or drop its stare.

"Get out of here, you stupid bird!" Alex yelled as he picked up his cup and the newspaper. Keeping one eye on the raven, he put the pen into his pocket and glanced at the finished crossword puzzle. His attention was drawn to the first entry, the one he'd struggled with, and he read the seven-letter word. For the briefest of moments, he tried to make a connection between the puzzle, the bird, and the voice, but the thought slipped away as he rose and walked into the house. Alex glanced back through the screen door when the raven quorked once and flew over the wall. He watched the bird disappear, and then he shook his head and walked down the hall to the bathroom to take a shower.

For the rest of the day, Alex managed to accomplish a number of tasks. He never did get into Sarah's closet to sort through all of her old stuff. That plan seemed to have vanished from his head like so many others did these days. Alex didn't think he was senile, but he'd be seventy-seven on his next birthday, and a little forgetfulness came with the territory.

For most of the thirty-six years they were married, Alex would drift off to sleep thinking about her even as Sarah lay next to him. That night, as he slid between the sheets, he brought up his favorite memory, the one of Sarah standing next to a desert willow on the edge of an arroyo. That hot day, they'd been hiking since sunrise. Sarah always took the lead, and he liked following her because it gave him a great view of her slim legs and trim hips. The wind was just strong enough to tug at the tree's leaves and blow her hair away from her cheek. As he stood behind her, she said his name almost as a sigh. He'd started to reach out to put his hand on her shoulder, but had stopped and stepped back when she raised her arms toward the sky and began singing, her whispery voice floating on the wind. The words and tune were unfamiliar to Alex, yet they were soothing. Bathed by the melody and the warm sun, he'd closed his eyes and breathed in the sound of her voice, the memory stirring his mind and his body. Over the years, he'd drawn on that memory when he was restless and had trouble falling asleep.

The next morning, when he opened his eyes, Alex could see the sunlight on the junipers. He heard the chittering of the birds and a barking dog from somewhere down the road. He stretched, moaned with the pleasure of a good night's sleep, and pulled the covers up to his chin. *He thought this would be a good day to stay in bed* as he looked at the closet door, but I really needed to get into Sarah's closet. Reluctantly, he flipped the blankets to the side and sat on the edge of the bed. He turned once to look at the closet door, then stood and headed for the kitchen.

Alex walked down the hill into town after he'd had his coffee and read the paper. He thought about all the years of hiking and eating natural food with Sarah. He'd kept on following her diet—which he called 'bark and twigs'—and occasionally, he'd have a beer with some of the guys from the hardware store. He even kept a bottle of tequila in the kitchen, one he and Sarah had used for special occasions. He remembered there hadn't been any of those for quite a while as he crossed the main street and headed for the deli on the corner.

The pleasant aroma of warm bread greeted Alex when he walked into the store. The guy behind the counter put a half-dozen slices of pastrami onto the scale, wrapped the meat in wax paper, and slid the package down the stainless-steel table to the girl at the cash register. He greeted the woman in front of Alex and asked if he could help her. Alex didn't hear what she said; he was bent over, looking through the glass cabinet at the variety of meats, trying to decide what he wanted. He was also trying not to stare at the woman's slim body and her tight workout pants. He shook his head and decided on the roast beef. The woman turned around as he stood back up and nearly bumped into him.

"Oh! I'm sorry," she said.

"No problem," replied Alex, stepping back out of the way. "It was my fault."

The woman smiled at him and whispered, "You should try the soup, it's wonderful." Alex watched her as she moved toward the door. Pushing it open, she turned and smiled at him again and then walked out into the bright sunlight.

"Can I help you?"

"Huh?" said Alex.

"What would you like to order, sir?"

"Uh, I'll have some of the soup," he said, still feeling the warmth of the woman's smile. He waited while the man filled the paper container, trying to remember the last time someone had flirted with him. *It must have been Sarah, and that was a long time ago*, he thought. Alex paid for the soup and a small loaf of sourdough bread and walked up the hill to his house, all the while thinking about the encounter with the woman. By the time he got home, though, he'd set the thought aside and felt ready to begin clearing out Sarah's closet.

Alex put the soup in the refrigerator, the bread in the old breadbox, and reluctantly walked down the hall to the bedroom, trying to forget about the dream. He took a deep breath and stared at the closet door, then took a step back and slumped down on the bed. Tears welled up in his eyes when he realized that the things in the closet were all he had left of Sarah and the time they'd had together. He knew that they were just clothes and shoes, but they were *her* clothes and *her* shoes, and giving them away would feel like cheating on her memory.

He closed his eyes and lay back on the bed. Tears ran down his cheeks. He thought about the day he and Sarah had moved into the house and how they'd unloaded the truck. They had sweated and cursed some of the tight corners. Eventually, they'd showered together when the truck was empty and made love on a sheet spread across the mattress. Alex choked back a sob and recalled that afterwards, they'd sat on kitchen chairs on the patio and drank half a bottle of tequila. They toasted their new house and their tired muscles and anything else that would allow them another shot of the liquor. That night, they'd laughed and told stories until the moon had made a full course across the sky. When the night revealed a cascade of stars on black velvet, they'd made one more toast and then rushed into the bedroom for another time of loving.

Sarah isn't her clothes and shoes, Alex thought. *She's my memories of her, and she's young and strong.* He sat up and looked at the door again, then rose and opened it. He expected to be hit with a cloud of dust; instead, he smelled Sarah's lavender oil. But the sweet memory of her softness and her beauty was suddenly interrupted by an icy chill that crept up his neck. Alex walked out of the closet and closed the door.

In the kitchen, he took the soup out of the refrigerator, poured it into a bowl, and put it in the microwave. *This is too weird*, he thought. *I'm just gonna sit outside, eat some soup and sourdough, and start acting like a grownup.* When the timer on the microwave went off, he carried the bowl, the bread, and the bottle of tequila out to the patio. The soup smelled good, like something Sarah might have made, yet as he sat back in his chair, he thought of the woman at the deli.

He filled the glass with the silver liquid and set it aside while he ate the bread and soup. When he finished, he stared at the shot glass, then picked it up and took several sips. After a few minutes, Alex's anxiety disappeared, and he took the dishes and the bottle back to the kitchen. He rinsed the bowl and the glass and put them in the sink. Then, grabbing the tall bottle, he took a deep breath and walked back down the hall into the bedroom.

A little anxious about what he might find, he opened the door to Sarah's walk-in closet and flipped on the light. The lavender smell was still there.

At first, each blouse or skirt he touched reminded him of Sarah, and he felt a trace of guilt when he took them off their hangers and carefully placed them on the bed. After struggling with some poignant memories, he finally worked his way through all of the hanging clothes and started pulling the large boxes from the shelves and the floor along the back wall. Most of the boxes were labeled in Sarah's familiar script. He carried the cartons two at a time and made a dozen trips to the front porch.

Alex returned to the bedroom to make sure the closet was empty and discovered he'd missed a shoebox pushed back into a far corner. He stretched up onto his toes, reached into the corner, and slid the box to the edge of the shelf. He was surprised by how light it was. When he lifted it down, he felt something slide inside the box, something small. Sarah had marked the outside with a single word—"Personal."

He stared at the word on the box, wondering why Sarah would have wanted to keep anything from him. *We always told each other everything. We had no secrets—except for this one, I guess.* Curious about the contents, he tucked the box under his arm, grabbed the tequila bottle, and returned to the kitchen. Walking out onto the patio, he heard the bill-tapping of the raven and spotted the bird perched high in a juniper across the wall but paid him no attention.

As he set the box on the table, he felt the fear of his dream again. Alex folded his arms across his chest and rocked the chair onto its back legs. The sun was still shining above the hill and tree line to the west, and Alex felt the sweat under his arms. His head was throbbing too, but he wasn't sure if it was because of the warm air or the half bottle of tequila he'd swallowed; *probably both*, he thought. He closed his eyes for a moment and tried to hang on to a memory that flitted into his mind like a hummingbird: something about Sarah and the sun and purple flowers. He reached out with his mind to grasp the thought, but it was slippery, and he couldn't hang onto it. Then, in an instant, he had it and followed the image to a memory of the first day he saw Sarah.

It had been in the summer, a few years after his divorce, and he'd gone with some buddies to an outdoor concert. They'd found a place at the back of the crowd with enough room to spread blankets on the lawn. The smell of flowers and pot floated on the soft breeze and the sounds of the band warming up seemed to glide alongside them. The voices of the growing crowd pulsated and rippled in waves, high and low, loud and soft, and the combination of the sounds and smells, and the beers they'd had gave Alex a wonderful buzz. With his legs stretched out in front of him, he leaned back on his elbows, closed his eyes and let the sunlight warm his face.

Somewhere inside his reverie, he sensed the slightest whiff of lavender; he took a deep breath and opened his eyes. Just down the slope, with her back to the stage, a woman was tossing pieces of bread to some chickadees that had gathered on the grass around her. She was tall and slender and was wearing a long dress of some delicate fabric. She'd pulled her shoulder-length hair away from her face and tied it in a ponytail and had slipped some small purple flowers above her ear. The faint scent of lavender caressed his senses, but it was her crystal blue, piercing eyes that touched him most. It felt as if she was looking through his eyes into the deepest part of him, as if she'd known him for all eternity. He wasn't afraid. Instead, he was so captivated by her that he rose and walked toward her, all the while trying to think of something cool to say; anything that wouldn't sound foolish. Her eyes never left his, and when he neared her, she extended her hand and said, "Hi, I'm Sarah."

"I'm Alex," he said, "and you're beautiful."

Sara hadn't blushed or laughed; she'd just smiled, looked at him, and said, "I knew you'd be here."

They ended up spending the afternoon together, and after the concert, he gave her a ride home. She gave him her phone number, and by fall, they were married.

The warm sun wouldn't let Alex stay in the daydream, so he opened his eyes and looked at the shoebox on the table. He poured himself another shot, then sat up straight in the chair, pulled the box square in front of him, and reached for the lid.

A whisper, "Don't touch the box."

Another frigid chill wrapped itself around his neck. *What's going on?* he thought. *That sounded like Sarah's voice. Is that what this is all about?* The raven quorked once, then spread its wings and flew from the juniper, lighting on the adobe wall at the back of the yard.

"What the hell," Alex said aloud. "There's that damned raven again." Then, turning away from the bird, he pulled the lid off the box and peered inside. What he saw was even odder than the raven.

The remaining sunlight reflected off a tiny silver hook and loop on the side of a small, hand-carved wooden box. The symbols scratched into the lid meant nothing to Alex, but maybe they had to Sarah. *Why else would she have kept it?* He sucked in a deep breath and exhaled slowly. He looked into the shoebox again and stared at the small box. *Why can't I touch it*, he thought. He tipped the shoebox and the smaller box slid out onto the table. Alex reached for it but stopped when the raven quorked loudly and flew toward him. The bird perched on the back of a chair not three feet from Alex.

Trembling in fear, Alex tried to keep his eyes on the raven, but the assault he'd made on the tequila bottle had taken a toll on his senses. His breathing had slowed, and his eyelids closed, like a curtain at the end of a play. He struggled to open them and to focus on the ebony bird. Alex fought the fatigue, but the liquor won the battle. His eyes closed again, his head relaxed, and his chin settled on his chest. The raven, perched as still as the Maltese Falcon, continued to stare at Alex through obsidian eyes.

Behind the darkness of his eyelids, something gnawed away in his head, urging him to fight, to open his eyes, to stay in the moment. He heard the great whooshing of a blacksmith's bellows and felt the pulsing wind on his cheeks. Alex forced his eyelids up and, through a tequila fog, looked directly into the red-rimmed eyes of the raven. The bird seemed as large as a condor, its giant wings spread in a wide arc, the feathers heavy, velvety, drape-like. It had left its perch on the chair and now stood beak to nose with Alex, its talons gripping the small box.

Alex wanted to back away, but the bird had him pinned to the chair. He tried to focus on the raven, struggling to draw a breath into his starving lungs but feared he'd startle the bird if he moved. Almost like a warning, the raven screeched, then pounded its wings and lifted off the table. Still holding the small box in its talons, it flew over the wall and disappeared beyond the junipers.

The sudden silence spread over Alex like a shroud, binding him to the chair, and mercifully, his mind went blank.

Alex woke up the next morning, surprised that he was in his bed and more surprised by the absence of a hangover. He rose quickly and walked out to the back yard, glancing at the junipers across the wall. The chair he'd been sitting in lay on its back, and the open shoe box and empty bottle were side by side on the small patch of grass just off the patio. He looked around the yard, trying to make sense of what he saw, but clarity wouldn't come, and soon he realized he didn't want to know what had happened. Instead, he decided that after a cup of coffee, he was going to take Sarah's stuff to the Rescue Mission and then head down the hill to the deli to see if there was anything going on, maybe buy some soup or make a new friend.

The Flesh of Domestic Animals Used as Food
by Chas Wilson

Dogtown wasn't much of a place, but it was all we had — hot, dry, and owned by Jarvis. It was a frontier place where laborers lived. Dairymen, small farmers, carpenters, masons, vineyard and field laborers, and truckers call Dogtown home now. A few leatherworkers, roofers, and small repairmen also live here. From time to time some of Jarvis' soldiers will stay at Florya's. Everyone watches these outsiders with fear and awe. We refer to them as outsiders, as we call the others who come and go, because they live by customs and traditions different from ours. Their lives are comfortable and prosperous in the sense that prosperity is understood in Dogtown and different. Food comes and goes to them, and they have real tables on which to eat. In Dogtown, those who share a cabin usually partake of a single dish from a single pot. It has become our custom to kneel around a low-placed tray and take food from the pot with metal spoons or even by hand. The only difference between the poorest and richest in Dogtown has nothing to do with our eating habits, but with the quality of food. Dogtown's poor eat boiled beans, roots, or wheat, with occasional bread. The better off get some meat. A slab of meat can turn the most dismal day into a holiday feast. Solidarity in Dogtown is expressed by bits of meat given to the needy by the more prosperous. Meat makes everyone's belly full, and everyone congratulates each other. When we have meat, we have peace. Meat is God's gift.

Dogtown has existed for over four years. When the war started, six years ago, all of Dogtown's inhabitants lived elsewhere. The war began when the armies from the east came across the frontier. We welcomed them at first. Our lives had been difficult for the forty years before the invasion. The Emperor had sent his soldiers and government officials into our land forty-six years ago and they were like salt, drying our blood. We paid high taxes and got nothing in return but indifference to our needs and disrespect to our culture.

So, when the invaders came and drove out the Emperor's army, they spoke to us in our own language and promised us prosperity and eventual self-government. We literally danced in the streets. We housed them, we fed them, our young men joined their army, and our young women danced with their soldiers. But our joy had a short life. Our young men were sent to the west to fight against the Emperor's army, and the invading soldiers stayed on and quickly began to ferret out and execute anyone thought capable of having or establishing a base of power.

When the news of our tribulations reached the ears of our young men in the west, many of them deserted the battles in the west and returned home. When they found their homes occupied or destroyed and their people enslaved, they sought the help of the Emperor's army, which provided them with arms and leaders. The leaders organized the young soldiers and all other able-bodied men into a people's army, which drove the invaders out.

Once the invaders were driven out, the emperor sent a much larger army to our land. This army of outsiders came back with a vengeance stronger than iron. They arrested or killed every able-bodied man who had participated in the war. Those arrested were sent to forced labor camps out west. We haven't heard or seen from any of them since.

The struggle for control of our land devastated it. When the Emperor's soldiers had control of us once again, they moved us from our homes and our shops and settled us in Dogtown, where they could better control us and use our skills to better support the war effort. The only ones left after the emperor regained control were women, children, and old and crippled men. I survived because I was crippled. I had an accident as a child that left me with a withered arm, a pronounced limp, and a milky eye.

Before Dogtown, I had been a bookseller in the city. What books the invaders and outsiders didn't burn, I managed to load into my garden cart and push here to Dogtown. Because I had no skills, I managed to convince the commandant of Dogtown that I could teach the children. I believe he allowed me to make my cabin a school because it occupied the young children's time. Without school, the mothers would have to care for them and thus couldn't work. If left on their own, the children became mischievous and unwieldy. When Jarvis replaced the commandant four months ago, I was allowed to continue educating the "beasties," as he called them, although he made them stop school and go to work once, they reached their tenth year. So, as long as there were children under ten, I was safe from execution. Otherwise, I would be dispatched as "without value."

One morning, not long after Jarvis came, as I washed myself before breakfast, the blanket covering my doorway was pushed aside, and Jarvis' woman walked in. She had her two little girls with her. "I am the wife of Commandant Jarvis," she said in the language of the outsiders, although she spoke it with an accent much different than theirs. "I want you to teach my daughters to read and write our language and to understand numbers. I have tried but I cannot make them understand."

I heard the story of Jarvis' woman from Florya, who heard it from one of the soldiers. One look at Jarvis' woman and the two girls made me believe it must be true. It is said that Jarvis rescued her from certain death when she was being beaten by her townspeople for having lain with the invading soldiers. She was tall, with thick yellow hair and eyes like robin eggs. Her skin was pale and, with the sun at her back in my doorway, she seemed to have an aura about her. Her daughters, on the other hand, were very dark, darker than my people. Their eyes were nearly black and revealed nothing. Their lips were flat, and their mouths closed tightly. They said nothing and looked ahead as if the past was dead and there was to be no future.

It is said that Jarvis' woman was raped by her townswomen with the handle of a hoe; the damage left her unable to bear children. After Jarvis took her, he allowed her to select two children from one of the refugee camps to be as her own. Florya said the impact of the war and the months of starving in the camps had left the two girls with dark skins and pale minds.

"This is Jinnah. She is seven. This is Teppa. She is five. Teach them what you can, but do not beat them." She said to me as she pushed each girl forward with her hands at their backs.

"I am honored, Jinnah's mother, to be considered worthy to teach your children. But your language is not my first, and I'm afraid I'm ill-equipped to do as you desire."

"I am told you are a learned man. I will make it worth your efforts." With that, she took the bag from her shoulder, opened it, and placed a large sausage on my bed. It must have weighed a kilo. For a man who has eaten boiled chicken meat but once in the last three months, the sausage seemed more valuable than the emperor's jeweled crown.

I babbled, lest she change her mind. "I will teach your children as well as I can, Jinnah's mother. However, given that I will be teaching them your language, I believe it will be too difficult to teach them at the same time as the other children. Perhaps you could bring them by at sundown each day and I could teach them then." She consented and said she would be back at sundown. I scarcely remember her leaving; my thoughts were awash with the promised pleasures of the sausage. I quickly cut a third of the sausage and, wrapping it in a shirt, hastened over to Florya's to share my wealth.

Florya is one of the poorest in Dogtown. She and her women exist on what the soldiers trade for a night of pleasure. Florya has very little, but she is quite generous. When a soldier gave her three chickens for a night spent with her women, Florya sent word for me to come to her cabin. When I arrived, one of the chickens was dressed and boiling in a pot. That was the last meat that I had eaten. Florya, the women, and I enjoyed our sausage together, and afterwards I read poetry to them. Florya especially liked the poetry of Ruto, who was from our land.

"He makes me remember the good times when I was a girl, before the emperor took our country. Your reading makes it seem as if he is here, whispering in my ear." With that, she wiped away a tear from her eye, brushed back her white hair, and said, "Now my friend, get back to your cabin. We have soldiers to entertain, and you have much to do, now that you have students both day and night."

At first, I struggled with the two girls, but soon they came to accept and trust me. Jinnah became a good student and challenged me daily. Teppa found it difficult to concentrate, but she tried very hard. Both pleased me with their efforts, and I told them so. Jinnah's mother always sat on my bed and watched me teach. She never spoke. She sat with her hands clasped in her lap, listened, and watched. Each night, when the lessons were finished, she helped the girls with their jackets and quietly left. There was always something left on my bed. Sometimes it was sliced meat wrapped in paper, sometimes ground meat wrapped in cabbage leaves, sometimes canned meat.

One night, late, after I had prepared my cabin for the next day's lessons, I lay in my bed, thinking about my good fortune. I heard the blanket at my door rustle and saw a figure standing in the darkness. In my fear, I whispered, "I have nothing. What do you want?"

"Shh, don't be afraid. It is I, Jinnah's mother." She moved toward me, took off her coat, and entered my bed. Everyone knows what a man and woman do, so I'll not elaborate. I am fifty-one years old and have only been with one woman before. Florya's women were put off by my arm and eye, and so refused to serve me. Florya, however, occasionally did and treated me kindly. Nonetheless, my times with Florya were nothing compared to that night with Jinnah's mother. That night, earth and heaven changed places. She left before dawn.

She came to me several nights thereafter, and we began to talk. I learned that she was twenty-seven and had worked in her widowed mother's dress shop. She said it was true that she had given herself to the commanding officer of the regiment which occupied her town. She said he was a kind old man. I wondered out loud if she wasn't afraid that Jarvis would discover us. "He won't. We sleep in different rooms, and he only comes to my room if he has killed someone that day. I always find out before he comes home at night if someone is killed. I don't come to you then."

One night, after Jinnah's mother had shared my bed, someone came into my cabin, but it wasn't Jinnah's mother. It was two men. One held a knife to my throat and spoke. The other stood at the doorway and peered through the space he made by pushing the blanket aside. "We know that you are bedding Jarvis' woman. Only God knows why she has chosen you. Jarvis has killed more of our people since he's been here than have died in the previous four years. He must be stopped. We want you to kill Jarvis."

I asked him how could I, a half-blind, old crippled bookseller, kill the terrible and powerful Jarvis? He has many soldiers with weapons and is always surrounded by his security squad.

"We have watched his house. When he goes in at night, the guards remain outside. His woman bribes them to allow her unrestricted passage. We want you to put a bomb in his bedroom."

"She has unrestricted passage, I haven't."

"This you'll have to work out."

Another night, as we lay in bed talking, I told her of my desire to see her place, "I want to be with you, among your things. I feel it will make me know you better." I was surprised when she said it was possible and somehow exciting. Jarvis was to go to the regional headquarters soon and would be gone for a night. She said that I could follow her and the girls to her home, and she could let me in through the root cellar. She was certain no one would see. If I left before dawn, no one would be the wiser. As we talked, she became more and more excited about the idea. "I'll show you pictures of my family and my town," she said. "I want you to know everything about me."

After she left, my two visitors returned. I told them of the plan, and they said the bomb would be ready. I wanted to be sure that the bomb wouldn't hurt her or the girls. The one who held the knife before responded, "It is not a very powerful bomb, so you must be certain to place it under his bed. If it doesn't kill him, he will kill us all. Before he does that, I will remove all of your skin while you are still alive. Don't worry about Jarvis' woman and the children. Worry about yourself. We will bring you the bomb before the sun rises." And they did. They returned when it was still dark and gave it to me. I know nothing of bombs, so they told me, "carry it this way" and "place it this way." I listened, and I learned.

That evening, as Jinnah's mother was removing the two girls' jackets, she whispered, "Tonight."

That night, as I was following them home, I stayed a distance away. Jinnah's mother thought it was so that I would not be seen near them. While that was true, more importantly, I did it so she wouldn't see the bomb. When I got to the root cellar door, I hid the bomb in the bushes before I tapped at the door.

She brought me inside and I was dazed by the opulence. The root cellar was crowded with food, enough to feed Dogtown for years. There were smoked meats and sausages hanging from the ceiling, and bins filled with potatoes, carrots, onions, and apples. There was a wall of shelves and each shelf was loaded with cans of meat and fruit, and jars of pickled vegetables.

She led me upstairs and showed me the room where guests are entertained, the girls' rooms, and Jarvis' room (which I quickly but carefully studied), and finally brought me to her room. It was several times larger than my cabin and had a variety of sofas, tables, and cabinets. At the end of the room, in the center of the wall, on the mantle above the fireplace, were two pictures, framed in silver. "This is my father; He died when I was thirteen. This is the building in which I was raised. Downstairs is the dress shop and upstairs is our apartment." Then she turned from looking at the pictures, held my hands in hers, and proclaimed, "My name is Chaya." Then she raised her head, looked into my eyes, and kissed me.

I left her sleeping, put my trousers on, and went down to the root cellar. I got the bomb and, doing exactly as I had been told, placed it under Jarvis' bed. I then returned to her room, got dressed, and slipped quietly out the root cellar door.

The bomb killed Jarvis as he slept the next night. Jinnah's mother and the girls were unharmed by it. When the Emperor's officials came, they determined that only Jinnah's mother had had access to the house during Jarvis' absence, so she must have been responsible. A summary court was held; she was found guilty and hanged from the scaffold in front of the mason's cabin. I never spoke a word in her defense.

The girls were sent to Dogtown. No one but Florya was willing to take them. Although I didn't have much, I soon took Jinnah from her, to live as my daughter. Teppa stayed at Florya's. Things are back to normal now in Dogtown. Jarvis was replaced by another outsider. There are still children to teach, so I've kept my job and my life. Jinnah and I haven't eaten meat for some time now. And the war? The war seems endless.

Henry and the Message on the Back of Sunny's Turkey
by Howard Wilson

Seven-year-old Henry liked to draw and took pains to do it as best he could. His first-grade teacher the year before had told his mom and dad that he was one of the few children who could show motion in his figures and that he had never drawn a blue line across the top of his pictures to stand for the sky.

Henry and his eight-year-old brother Larry often spent weekend afternoons at the dining table, drawing. It could be soldiers, cowboys, or the Three Stooges, but they would be engrossed for more than an hour; at intervals, one of the boys would show the other what he had done. Their older brother, Jack, was an accomplished artist nearly thirteen years old and the younger kids wanted to be as good as Jack was when they reached his age.

Henry and Larry had to be thrifty with the paper as it was not easy to come by. Their dollar-a-week allowance only went so far and after buying Cokes, candy, and comic books, little was left over and good unlined paper wasn't cheap. Occasionally, their mom would bring home end sheets of data processing paper from her job where she worked as an accounting clerk. Their collection of worn-out pencils and stubby crayons was kept in a sixteen-millimeter film reel can and supplying it with new stock was also a challenge.

Naturally, there were abundant supplies at John Marshall Elementary where Henry was in the second grade, but they were to be used only in school and only during the time assigned to art. Fortunately, Henry liked school and was good or better in all his subjects (not including anything physical, as he was generally uncoordinated.) He was no model student, however, as his grade report reflected poorly on his "personal habits and attitudes." That is to say, he needed to "show self-control," to "work carefully," and to "show thrifty use of time and materials." Henry displeased his teachers by talking out of turn and he was not always "considerate of the rights of others."

It may have been that Henry was impatient to learn faster than his fellow pupils, but in any event, showing self-control was something he had not mastered by early November of his second-grade year. Someone might blame his behavior on being the youngest of six bright kids — an attention-getting device. It wasn't easy being heard at the dinner table when everyone was talking at once.

Henry had his romantic side. As far back as when he was four, he felt an attraction to his next-door neighbor Cathy, who was seven. He confessed his ardor to his sister Cleo, who was Cathy's age, and Cleo betrayed Henry to the neighbor girl, much to the little boy's embarrassment. In kindergarten, Henry developed a crush on a classmate, Linda, a cute little girl in his room, and told his other sister, Carmen, how he felt. Carmen told Cleo and both girls thought it was so cute and made so much of it that Henry was abashed and kept his crushes to himself from then on.

In first grade, his crush was a porcelain-skinned blonde named Dianne, and Henry would imagine her as the subject of every sweet, romantic love song emanating from the radio. Toward the end of the school year, his secret attentions shifted to Sunny, another blonde with short hair and bangs. Whereas Dianne was quiet and studious, Sunny was perky and playful. Both types appealed to the kid.

One afternoon, during the lunchtime recess, Henry was chasing Sunny around the playground. It was a popular pastime for boys to chase girls and never catch them. It was also good exercise. As Henry was keeping his distance, Sunny abruptly halted, held her hand up like a traffic cop, and asked Henry to wait a second. "I have to pull my underpants up," she told him.

Henry was too embarrassed to continue the chase; he smiled ruefully and walked away, thinking that things had gone too far with Sunny. Somehow, she had crossed the line, and he could no longer look at her the same way. For the rest of the school year and into summer, Henry's affections were directed towards movie and TV goddesses and the occasional teenage neighbor girl.

In September, when school resumed, Henry found that Sunny was in his second-grade class. He had nearly forgotten his attachment to her; by now, she was just one of the girls in Mrs. Gretsch's schoolroom. At that point, Henry had not selected any particular girl to be his secret crush, and the task of adapting to a new teacher and new rules, along with new subjects, took up most of his attention.

One innovation that Mrs. Gretsch introduced to the class was the Calendar. A large calendar full of red-letter dates was posted on one of the corkboards in the room. For September, Mrs. Gretsch had placed a large picture of a schoolboy and a schoolgirl in front of a school bell. The drawing looked like the cover of a magazine and was probably *inspired* by the cover of a magazine.

"Now, class, for October and the rest of the months of the year," the teacher announced, "I will want you to submit your drawings of artwork for the calendar. The winner will have his or her work of art displayed above the calendar for the entire month and will also get a free ice cream bar on ice cream day each Friday during the month. Isn't that a nice reward?"

Henry liked the idea of winning a Popsicle and of having his artwork displayed and he responded to the challenge with an ambition he seldom felt. There were three weeks left in September, and the October calendar picture would likely have something to do with Halloween. Henry loved Halloween, loved dressing up, and mostly loved all the free candy that came with the holiday. Then there was the Halloween Kiddie Parade down Lincoln Avenue in downtown Anaheim, which was a highlight of the school year when all the kids in the city would dress up and show themselves to the residents and merchants who gathered to see them. Halloween had always been big in Anaheim for nearly half a century, and as it grew from a small town to a big city, the October festivities grew along with it. There was no doubt that Halloween would be the subject of the next schoolroom calendar.

For homework assignments associated with art, the children were allowed to take sufficient amounts of pencils, paper, and crayons or coloring pencils home with them, so Henry was not dependent upon his meagre supply to achieve his artistic goal. After careful consideration, he determined that his Halloween picture would incorporate the Three Stooges somehow. By the end of the month, he had worked up a large colored drawing of Larry as the Wolfman, Moe as Dracula, and Curly as Frankenstein's Monster, standing side-by-side-by-side in a graveyard with bats flying all around and the full moon above. He told himself, "This is so good, it even scares *me*."

Henry felt confident that his picture would be the winner. The competition appeared to be a series of black cats, jack-o-lanterns, amorphous ghosts, and witches on broomsticks. The same old stuff. There were a few skeletons, but they looked like stick figures and not the sort of deathly scary creatures that would cause nightmares. It was a cinch that he would win, Henry thought.

It wasn't a cinch. He lost. It may have been the originality of his project; it may have been that it was too scary; it may even have been that Mrs. Gretsch hated the Three Stooges. It never occurred to Henry that it may not have been such a good picture. In any event, a girl named Karen won the prize with her crowded scene incorporating every possible Halloween icon, including a scarecrow and a slightly three-dimensional haunted house made of construction paper. Henry suspected that Karen's mother had a hand in the project. Mrs. Gretsch made a big deal about

Karen's collage and handed back the rest of the entries with the offhand comment that she thought everyone's effort was satisfactory. Henry was disappointed but decided that his project would be perfect for November.

The month of October brought with it the leaves turning brown from green without any golds, oranges, or yellows in between, unlike the pictures of autumn in the storybooks and readers the children learned from. Southern California weather was nothing like the rest of the country, and the only snow Henry ever saw was on the mountains north of Anaheim when it rained, and the smog was cleared away temporarily. Meanwhile, the city was gearing up for Halloween, but a large part of Henry's mind was already on Thanksgiving because he knew that the November calendar would inevitably be about that holiday.

Henry's mid-term grade card was pretty much like the ones he had received in the first grade. No letter marks like A's, B's, or C's would be given to the lower graders, but instead, "Satisfactory for This Child," "Needs to Improve," or "Has Shown Improvement." His academic marks were satisfactory except, of course, penmanship and physical education, but his work habits and social habits generally needed lots of improvement. Nothing was mentioned about art.

Toward the end of October, when the assigned materials were distributed to the pupils, Henry was eager to set to work. It was his intention to create a masterpiece guaranteed to cause everyone's mouth to water who looked at it. It would be a huge roast turkey in simmering gravy with the stuffing pouring out of the cavity and wavy lines representing steam rising above it. He would use colored pencils instead of crayons to get more of the subtleties of tone his work demanded. When finished, he set his tools down and admired his creation. Henry felt deep in his heart that the golden bronze beauty he had made was a sure winner.

The entries were due on Friday, the 28th of October, and the winner would be announced on Tuesday, the first. As Henry's competitors dropped off their entries, he was pleased to see tired old Pilgrims and Indians, traced from school textbooks, cornucopias filled with foodstuffs cut from *Look* magazine, and an abundance of turkeys on the hoof in a variety of colors not found in nature. Some of the entries looked too good and were probably creations of a parent or older sibling.

Even though the wonders of Halloween would intervene for a couple of days, Henry was looking forward to the first of November, assuring himself that his turkey would grace the calendar until it was time to make with the Christmas/Hanukkah display. A month with free ice cream bars or frozen pops every Friday seemed assured.

The kiddie parade went well and that night, trick-or-treating paid of abundantly with load of candy and only a few untrustworthy popcorn balls and home-baked cookies to toss into the trash. A certain portion of the haul of each of the four younger Valentine children still in grade school was tossed into a communal bowl, so that junior high schoolers Brad and Jack could have some share in the bounty. Henry contributed a generous amount of Dum Dums, Smarties, Abba Zabbas, and Good 'n' Plenty while keeping back anything with chocolate. Carmen, Cleo, and Larry did the same. With Halloween all but over, Henry dreamed of the triumph that would be his on the following day.

"Attention, class," Mrs. Gretsch said when the class took their seats following the Pledge of Allegiance. "I'm going to announce the winner of the calendar contest for November." Then she held up Sunny's entry. Henry could not believe what he was seeing. It was a mixed-media representation of a turkey on the hoof: Sunny used pencil, watercolors, and construction paper. To Henry's eyes, Sunny's turkey looked no better or worse than the dozen other turkeys entered, and besides that, as far as he knew, his was the only baked bird on a platter presented for consideration. What a gyp!

Henry brooded throughout the first lessons leading up to morning recess and was unusually quiet for someone known to speak out of turn and talk to his neighbor. He looked over at smiling, triumphant Sunny and wondered what it was that he ever saw in her. Her face looked stupid, her bangs looked stupid, her dress was foolish, and, he recalled, she couldn't keep her underpants up. How could she have won?

Instead of lining up to ride the swings as was his habit, Henry sat down on the grass and thought of the injustice that had been done to him. When ice cream day rolled around, he would have to put up the dime for his treat and it would be a reminder that the prize he felt was his had been unjustly snatched from his hands. A few minutes later, Sheldon and Adam, guys from his room, came down and sat next to him. The two boys were not the best or best-behaved pupils, and each had been sent to the principal's office at least a few more times than Henry had. His first-grade teacher and

Mrs. Gretsch both believed that Henry's behavior would improve if he cultivated the friendship of nicer boys like Timothy or Frank, higher achievers with good conduct marks. Henry liked Tim and Frank well enough, but he liked the other guys as well. They had something different to offer.

"What are you doing sitting here, Henry?" Adam asked, wiping his nose on his jacket sleeve.

"I don't feel like playing now. I'm mad."

It was Sheldon's turn. "What are you mad for?"

"Mrs. Gretsch gave it to Sunny, the calendar prize and mine was better. Didn't you think that mine was better?"

"Yeah, yours *was* better. Girls always get the favors, you know. Especially girls like Sunny, who are always sweet-sweet to the teachers." Sheldon pretended to barf. "They make me sick."

"What can you do?" Adam started to get back up again.

"You can't do nothing," was Sheldon's answer. "Like my dad says, sometimes the deck is stacked against you. He says that all the time." Henry didn't care to accept Sheldon's dad's philosophy, as his envy and malice kept him occupied for the rest of the morning and into lunchtime. He hardly tasted his baloney sandwich, corn chips, and the little box of raisins, and as soon as Rachel, the sixth grader doing duty as table monitor, excused him, Henry began to wander aimlessly toward the classroom.

Mrs. Gretsch was no doubt grabbing a smoke with the other teachers in the faculty lounge, so the classroom was unattended. With this in mind, Sheldon and Adam had no difficulty in persuading Henry to enter the room with them.

Taking other seats than the ones assigned to them, the three kids looked around, enjoying being in the classroom without all the other pupils and the commanding presence of Mrs. Gretsch. Eventually, the topic of the day presented itself as they gazed upon Sunny's turkey, a misshapen color wheel hovering over the thirty days of November and making Henry's anger and resentment rise again to their heights.

"That Sunny is such a ninny," Sheldon said.

"I can't stand teachers' pets," Adam rejoined. He stepped over to the corkboard and yanked the picture off."

"Hey!" Henry suddenly felt afraid. "What are you doing? Don't wreck it."

"You know what we should do?" Sheldon was grinning. "We should write something on the back and stick it back up again, so nobody knows what we did."

"Write? Like what?" Adam carried the picture of the turkey over to Mrs. Gretsch's desk and laid it face down. He grabbed a pencil and paused, looking from one boy to the other.

Sheldon smiled and stuck his right finger up into the air as if he had the idea of a lifetime. "What about 'Sunny is full of shit?'"

Henry was surprised. He had never heard any of his friends say "shit" before; only his dad, his mom occasionally, his dad's friends, and some older boys he was afraid of. "No! Write 'Sunny is full of farts,'" he suggested as a more acceptable alternative.

Adam ended up writing SUNNY IS FULL OF SHIT AND FARTS, and seemed satisfied with his composition, tacking the bird back onto the board in as near its original position as he could manage. "That should do it," Sheldon said. Henry's first thoughts were that he had avenged himself of the wrong wrought by Sunny and Mrs. Gretsch.

The three boys looked out of the classroom door to see if any teacher could spot them leaving the unattended classroom, but the coast was clear, although Henry did notice little Rosita, who was in their class, glance briefly in their direction. None of them thought anything of it.

There were only a few minutes left before the freeze bell would ring, so Henry and his friends returned to the playground and climbed onto the monkey bars. "Don't say anything to anybody about this," Sheldon warned. Both Adam and Henry nodded conspiratorially, and when the time came, the three boys filed back into the classroom.

The rest of the afternoon did not go well with Henry. The temporary feeling of satisfaction at having participated in the defacement of Sunny's prize turkey gave way to a sense of shame and fear of discovery. *What if he had won the prize and somebody else did to his turkey what they did to Sunny's? What if Sunny takes the turkey home in December without looking at the back and her parents see the message? How would he like that to happen to* him*? What kind of boy does a trick like that to a girl?* Having been tempted into revenge, Henry was now being tempted into confession.

Henry then wondered what Adam and Sheldon would do to him if he squealed. Who would be friends with a guy that squealed? Henry looked over at Sheldon and Adam, and they seemed unconcerned about what they had done. There was no sign of a troubling conscience with either of them.

Mrs. Gretsch had assigned silent reading, and the two boys were bent over their storybooks. Henry was up to date on his assignments and was supposed to be doing supplemental reading in a Nancy Drew mystery, but he just stared at the page. Nobody saw him with Sheldon and Adam. He wouldn't mention their names. He would just take the blame himself.

Suddenly, as if on impulse, Henry leaped from his seat, crying out, "I'm sorry! I'm sorry!" and yanked Sunny's turkey off the wall and tossed it to the ground. Amid the gasps, chattering, and commotion, Mrs. Gretsch picked up the turkey and looked at Henry, thinking that his envy had got the better of him. Then she noticed the writing on the back and told Henry to sit at the foot of her desk.

"What is the meaning of this, Henry? Did you write this?"

Unable to speak through his sobbing, Henry just nodded.

"Well, it doesn't look like your handwriting." Then to the pupils, "Quiet down, class. Yes, Rosita?"

"Mrs. Gretsch? I saw Henry in the room with Adam and Sheldon during lunch."

"You two," the teacher said, furrowing her brow and pointing at one then the other, indicating that Henry's friends should join him in front of the class. "I suppose you think this was funny. Well, it's not. Boys your age shouldn't be using this kind of language. Boys of *any* age shouldn't use those words."

Sheldon and Adam kept their heads down, not from shame, but to conceal from Mrs. Gretsch the fact that they were smirking. They each cast sidelong glances at Henry, with Sheldon pretending to blubber and Adam sneering. At least Henry didn't implicate them all by himself.

"You should all be ashamed of yourselves," Mrs. Gretsch said. "At least Henry showed that he felt shame for something he knew was wrong. I should send you up to Mr. Depew, but I'm not going to and you two can thank Henry for that. You would be better off if you were as ashamed as he is." Mr. Depew was the school principal, and Henry dreaded having to go to his office, something he had been able to avoid so far this school year. It was said that repeated offenses would lead to getting swats from a ping pong paddle, something that frightened Henry more than anything.

Mrs. Gretsch sent the boys back to their desks. "I'm going to erase this filthy message from the back of Sunny's turkey, and we will say no more about what happened today." She pulled out her big pink eraser and began scrubbing away so that soon, the message was gone. "But I want us all to remember to act like good human beings and to treat one another with respect. This must not happen again." She looked from child to child as she gave this speech and Henry returned her look through teary eyes and vowed to himself that he would be what his teacher wanted him to be. He still talked out of turn, disturbed his neighbors, and turned in messy work. Some things come naturally to boys like Henry. But never again did he seek revenge on another person out of sheer envy.

Mandy
by Bruce Wilson

I steal, and I have been stealing for as long as I can remember. I don't know how or when it started, and even that's not important now. I spoke these words out loud, but my voice was muted, the sound swallowed by the cinderblock walls.

Across the metal table—the one with the iron loop that bound my handcuffed wrists—sat a man who didn't respond to my statement. His face was putty-like, dull, and scarred; his cheeks were puffy and his nose showed evidence of having been broken at least once. He was a cop, of course, but an old-fashioned one. His clothes were worn; the collar of his once white shirt was stained yellow, and his paisley tie held reminders, evidence, I suppose, of his last few meals. The cop's eyes, however, were alert. The irises were an unremarkable brown, but the whites were—white, clean, bright, brilliant white. These eyes belonged on a Hollywood cop, a handsome, well-dressed, intelligent, bound-for-the-chief's-office kind of police officer. The cop's hair-filled ears may not have heard what I said, but I knew that his eyes did. They knew what I said and what I didn't or couldn't say.

He watched my lips move and my nostrils flare as I breathed in the stale air of the interrogation room. His eyes seemed to collect and catalog the stubby two-day whiskers on my face, the shadows on the soft underlids of my eyes, and the old crescent-shaped scar on my chin.

In my second hour in the cube-shaped room, I began to believe he would never ask me a question because he wouldn't need to. He had, I believed then, the ability to read what was going on in my brain. He had likely read the booking report and would, therefore, know my name and address since all of that information was on my driver's license. Yet, I think he knew those things anyway.

I probably won't even have to confess anything or explain how I got caught inside the shop after it was closed. This guy already knows everything about me.

I closed my eyes for a moment, wondering if by doing this it would force him to talk, to actually use his mouth and tongue and lips, to finally get with the program and interrogate me and ask me questions I could ignore. He didn't. I peeked once to see if he'd moved or turned his head, but he was still gazing at my face. I stopped peeking, but it was too late. Even with my eyes squeezed shut, I could feel his glowing eyes moving through my head like a law student searching the library stacks, like a deal-driven female shopper touching every garment on the Nordstrom's sale rack. His eyes were scanning my mind, looking for clues, evidence, signs and symbols of my guilt.

Before I knew it, I sensed that he'd seen, with his all-knowing eyes, how I'd picked the back door lock and pushed my way into the building. His presence in my head wrapped around my memory of the cluttered stock room, the fly-swarmed pizza box and the shopkeeper's apron hanging from a hook. He saw me open the interior door, pause at the entrance to the store and gaze around the room, looking for the more expensive, more easily pawned items. In my mind's eye, I saw him smile as the red and blue lights of a police cruiser flashed against the grimy front window. If he knew all of this, I wondered, then, why I was sitting in this stale, gray cube instead of defending myself in a cell crowded with drunks, muggers, and car thieves.

I opened my eyes with a start. The mush-faced cop hadn't moved. He still stared at me with his unblinking, silver-white eyes. That's when I realized that he could only see my experiences, my memories, my history. He could not know the future. His eyes saw only what once was. At first, I was relieved, almost convinced that I had nothing to fear, until I realized that the cop would have unlimited access to everything I had ever said or done, knowledge of every place I had ever been. That's when I knew I was in trouble. He would know about my dreams from junior high, the ones where I'm invisible and make trips into the girls' locker room at school. He would *see* me sneaking a look at Howie's paper during a History final. He would watch as I filled in the blanks on my tax return with false information. I wasn't sure how I could stop him from going there, especially since these thoughts had just now been resurrected. What was I going to do? How could I block mister know-it-all cop from digging any further and deeper into my now guilt-ridden memories?

Then, an idea, disjointed as it was, began to tickle the edges of my thoughts. Hints of a solution skimmed through my brain cells, settling in the cracks and crevices, looking for something to pull them into a fully formed solution.

By focusing on the officer's face, I seemed able to hold his searching eyes in place, like a triangular yellow yield sign, slowing his access and giving time for the idea to reveal itself. If I was going to keep him out of those dark, secret places, I'd need a thoroughly effective solution that would end his probing or at least force him to revert to using his voice. When the idea arrived on the screen in my head, I didn't immediately recognize its brilliance. But I realized I had no choice; it was the only idea there, the only one that might work.

So, I started humming one of the worst songs ever created—first, just the melody, the sounds, the rising and falling notes. The cop started to tap his fingers on the table, picking up the beat, his eyebrows joining in as well.

He tried to look away, but it didn't work. The lyrics revealed themselves in moments and grew along with the song into a full-fledged, all-out, balls-to-the-wall earworm. Over and over, I pushed it along, and soon enough, it took up a life of its own. The cop's eyes were still in my head, but they were shuddering, blinking, almost quaking. It seemed as if they were seeking a way out of my brain.

At the same time, the cop's face looked as if it was melting, sagging even more. Sweat dripped from his scalp and coursed down his forehead and along the creases at the edge of his bulbous nose. His lower lip quivered, and a stream of drool leaked out of the right side of his mouth. The strangest change, though, happened, as you might have guessed, with his eyes. The dull brown irises took on a walnut-hued luster as the whites faded to a dull, lifeless, old banana yellow.

The man scooted his unpadded steel chair away from the table, stood slowly and unsteadily, then turned toward the door. He looked in my direction, but clearly, he wasn't focused on me. He tapped twice on the door, and as it opened, he stumbled out of the room and began singing, almost gagging out the words...

<pre>
    Well you came and you gave without taking
        But I sent you away, oh Mandy
   Well you kissed me and stopped me from shaking
        And I need you today, oh Mandy

    Well you came and you gave without taking
        But I sent you away, oh Mandy
    You kissed me and stopped me from shaking
             And I need you...
</pre>

© Scott English and Richard Kerr

Tripoli
by Chas Wilson

Rocky had just worked a double shift and was having trouble keeping his eyes open. He had been to the laundromat before his first shift started, so he had been going for over 18 hours. He was beat! Ten more minutes of driving, and he would be home. He cheered himself up with the thoughts of all that tomato-season overtime. The cannery would pay him for twenty-two hours even though he had only worked sixteen. He was saving every penny that he could. He had big plans for his future and wasn't going to squander this opportunity to make his fortune. Nothing was going to derail him from making a lot of money and becoming somebody!

He started to nod off to sleep when he was jerked awake by his ancient Volkswagen humping and bumping off the road and onto the shoulder. He braked to a stop.

"Jeez, I thought you were going to run me over! Anyway, thanks for stopping." A young woman wearing a bicycle helmet was cradling something in what appeared to be a shirt of some kind. He thought it must have been her shirt since she was wearing a bra but no shirt. Despite the adrenaline coursing through his veins, little of it had reached his over-tired brain, and he was still somewhat in a dream state.

"I was out for a ride and like I got a flat and when I was sitting down kinda looking at my tire I heard like a mewing sound and it was coming from a big paper sugar bag but when I opened the bag I found like a bunch of eggshells and snails and this little kitten inside and she was like moving and mewing and then she stopped doing anything and so I kinda wrapped her in my shirt and figured I didn't have time to fix the flat and so I started waving at the cars and you stopped and we need to like take her to the animal hospital or something!"

Rocky tried to keep up with all the words she machine-gunned at him, but could only get out, "I don't know where a people hospital is, let alone an animal hospital." He didn't add that he had no time for hysterical girls and that all he really wanted to do was go home and sleep.

"I got it on my phone. Can we take my bike too? I don't want to leave it here."

His VW bug came with a roof rack when he bought it, so he swung the bicycle up and secured it to the rack with a couple of bungee cords she had in her bicycle's basket. She was in his field of vision when he was securing the bicycle, and he was having difficulty concentrating on the task at hand. He had seen much more skin on the tourists who came into his parents' souvenir shop back home, but on this morning, he was definitely distracted by her flawless pale skin. "I have some clean t-shirts in the baskets in the back. Perhaps you would care to put one on."

"Oh yeah, sorry. Thanks! That's so sweet. Hey, you have kind of an accent. I'm Emily. What's your name? Where are you from? Just go straight on this road for a mile and a half."

"Everyone calls me Rocky. I'm from Trinidad."

"I'm not very good with Geology…that's kinda between Hawaii and New Zealand. Right?"

He was having trouble gauging her seriousness and keeping up with her speech delivery, so he responded with a weak, "I suppose one could say that."

"So, what brought you here? Turn left at the light."

"My sister married an executive at Intel in Folsom. He sponsored my immigration. I don't have much computer acumen, so I got a job in the label room at the cannery."

"D'you like it here? I don't. I'm thinking about moving to France or Cleveland. Take the next right."

"I like it here very much. In fact, I want to stay and become a citizen one day."

"You see what they did to this little kitty? People who did this are…there on the right."

He pulled into the parking area and hadn't even come to a stop before she was out of the bug and into the hospital. Now what? Stay? Leave the bike and go home? After a few moments, he followed her in and saw her disappearing around a corner right after he opened the door. He sat down and picked up a four-year-old copy of "People" magazine, and he fell asleep in a few moments. He was awakened when he heard her raising her voice.

"What do you mean I can't take her until I've paid? I *told* you I would bring the money back later." She turned to Rocky, "They won't let me take Tripoli home!" He mouthed the word "Tripoli?" without making a sound. "Yeah, I named her in honor of your country and because she has three white feet. Isn't she cute?"

Despite wondering what he was doing here in the first place, he approached the counter and asked how much it would cost to release the kitten and if they would accept his credit card. The receptionist looked at his card and said, "Rakesh Patel." Then she pushed the card into a machine and asked, "Which one is your last name?" He told her. "OK, the transaction went through, so the account for Tripoli Patel is paid."

"Thanks everyone, for fixing my kitty! Thank you, Rocky! Come on, let's go." Once outside, she said to him, "You are so sweet! You also look pretty tired. You want to get a coffee or something?"

Tired – no. Exhausted – yes, and wondering what he was doing with this girl! "Yes, I am rather tired. I think I would like that, although I prefer tea."

"I know the best place to get tea – English Breakfast, Irish Breakfast, Earl Gray, Dar-something. Anyway, they charge by the number of bags in the cup, not the size of the cup. Cool, huh? They're right next to where I work; I'm a cashier at Toasty Buns. You know, Burgers and stuff."

So they went to "Cuppa," next door to "Toasty Buns." Once inside, he found that she knew everyone inside, all the staff and every customer. She introduced Rocky to everyone and told them what a wonderful person he had been this morning. One customer introduced to Rocky as "Doctor Bike" agreed to take her bicycle down to his shop and repair the tire. He was back before their tea was cool enough to drink. "The chain gang put Our Emily's machine ahead of all others. Good as new!"

They sat and drank a lot of tea, and Emily touched his arm often when she was emphasizing something she had said. Rocky needed to go but wanted to stay. He finally said that he must get home and get some rest; he had to go back to work later that day. Emily said, "Wait, hand me your phone." She typed a number into his phone, which caused hers to vibrate. She clicked hers off and handed him back. She leaned in, kissed his cheek, and said, "Promise you'll call me," then took Tripoli out to her bicycle, put her hand with thumb and pinky extended up to her ear, and mouthed to Rocky, "Call me." She put Tripoli in the basket and pedaled away.

Somehow, Rocky managed to stay awake long enough to get home. He had to be back at work in just under four hours. He set all three of the alarms he had, just in case. The caffeine in the tea didn't keep him awake.

However, three hours later, the water in the tea helped awaken him. As he was walking to the bathroom, he grabbed his phone and began muttering about a "crazy, beautiful dream." In the bathroom, he looked in the mirror and saw the lipstick on his cheek. Smiling, he looked down at his phone, and there was a text message from Emily that said, "Thinking about you. Call me."

He paused for a brief moment and considered his plans for the future and his fortune. Where one's heart is, naturally enough, will also be his treasure. He called her.

Henry And The Course Of Human Events
by Howard Wilson

Nine-year-old Henry almost always did what his ten-year-old brother Larry asked him to. Not because he was afraid of Larry, but because Henry was generally amiable and willing. Now, if Larry *told* him to do something, more often than otherwise Henry would have balked, resulting in a quarrel. The two brothers were close but not a single day ever passed that a fight did not erupt. Larry was a demanding playmate and sometimes forgot to say "please."

One Saturday afternoon in early November, when the boys were lying in their bunks after lunch, Larry remembered something. "Mrs. Lynn gave us an assignment yesterday, and I have to memorize something by next Friday."

"What do you have to memorize?"

"Well, we're learning about the Revolution now, and she wants us to memorize the Declaration of Independence."

"The whole thing?"

"No, just the first part. Let me get it." Larry rolled out of his bunk and stepped over to the desk the two boys shared with their two older brothers, Brad and Jack. He pulled a sheet of ditto paper that was tucked into his history book and held it up to show Henry.

"Let me get my glasses on," Henry said, getting up. Henry had only started to wear glasses the summer before and was not quite used to them. He was the fifth of the six Valentine kids to have them, Larry being the only member of the brood not afflicted with nearsightedness.

The typewritten sheet began, "When in the course of human events it becomes necessary for one people to dissolve the political bands which have connected them with another…' and went on from there. It ended with the words, "… than to right themselves by abolishing the forms to which they are accustomed."

"That's all? That's not the whole thing, is it?" Henry's fourth-grade classroom at John Marshall Elementary School had a replica of the Declaration on the wall; he could tell it had many more words than he was looking at.

"It's enough. I was going to ask you. Would you help me memorize it? Please. It's not like you're doing anything now."

It was slow going, but by the end of the week, they both had it memorized. The meaning of the text became a subject of conversation and private contemplation because the wording was in a style unfamiliar to boys who were accustomed to reading family encyclopedias, school textbooks, young persons' fiction, and comic books. The phrase "all men are created equal" seemed to Henry to be "self-evident" in one way but questionable in another since he knew that he was more equal in intelligence and less equal in sports and good looks than some of the boys in his fourth-grade class. Even Larry was faster and more coordinated and a handsomer kid than Henry ever figured he'd be. He had heard one of his sisters' friends comment on his "goofy baby face." The pale, gray-rimmed spectacles and buzzed hairdo did not help his appearance at all.

Henry was by nature *a romantic kid*. The tabletop radio tuned to KFWB in their bedroom would play love songs by Brenda Lee and Ricky Nelson among the dance numbers and novelty tunes, and after having seen Elvis Presley and Tuesday Weld in *Wild in the Country*, Henry wanted to *be* Elvis romancing Tuesday. He spent the rest of the day after the matinee walking around his backyard by himself, trying to keep the emotion of love in his heart.

At the same time, Henry had borne secret crushes on his older brother's high school girl acquaintances, on glamorous TV actresses, and even on one or two girls in his classroom. Henry could not remember a time when he did not like looking at pretty girls. Neither was he above peeking into his dad's "men only" adventure magazines with their photographic layouts of strategically draped models. It is enough to say that Henry liked girls as much as any nine-year-old boy, maybe more.

Henry's mom and dad had joined a bowling league at Anaheim Bowl that fall, and, as usual, the two younger boys would accompany them to the alley on any Friday night when the teenage older brothers were not going to be home. Brad and Jack would have their own plans, and the junior high school-age sisters, Carmen and Cleo, were both regular babysitters. Anaheim Bowl had a nursery of sorts where grade school kids were dropped for supervised play while their parents rolled strikes and gutters, smoked, and drank bottle beer.

In some ways, the Anaheim Bowl nursery was overtime school for Henry since the lady who supervised the children was a grade school teacher in the Centralia district. Not that Henry didn't like Mrs. Romero, who was a fair and gracious middle-aged lady despite looking tired most of the time she watched kids on Friday nights. The nursery was equipped with a small playground outside featuring a swing set, slide, monkey bars, and a glider. It appealed more to the kindergartners and lower-grade children. The shelves on one side of the rather large room were stocked with Little Golden

Books, cast-off *Weekly Readers*, used coloring books, and a few Hardy Boys and Nancy Drew mysteries that nobody was ever seen reading. On the other side were donated toys, many the worse for wear, others in decent condition. Then there were the games boards: Parcheesi, checkers, Chutes and Ladders, and the rest, not all of which were complete as far as game pieces were concerned. Within a few minutes of the kids settling in for the long wait till their parents were ready to leave, the place was chaos.

Most nights at the bowling alley, Henry and Larry would keep each other company, but on this particular Friday, Larry saw a couple of guys from the sixth grade that he knew and decided to be with them instead, leaving Henry to amuse himself. The three boys went outside to the playground to talk about whatever it was that was worth talking about and Henry sat down listlessly, gazing without interest at the room full of kids. A brother-and-sister act, two redheads, asked Mrs. Romero if they could stand on one of the tables and sing "I'm Looking Over a Four-Leaf Clover" to the captive audience. Mrs. Romero said that she might organize a talent show later.

Then she had to break up a scuffle between two kindergartners who were both trying to take possession of the last uncolored page in one of the ragged coloring books.

Henry looked from one kid to another and then stopped on the face of a girl about his age. He took a quick breath. In his eyes, she was beautiful. Her features were perfect, and she wore her dark auburn hair in a pixie cut. Her eyes were brown and her permanent teeth didn't stick out in every direction the way Henry's were beginning to do. As far as Henry was concerned, the girl was one hundred times prettier than a girl in his class named Sally whom he kind of liked, and this Venus in the nursery was right up there with Tuesday Weld.

She was looking at the toys with very little interest. There was no way that Henry could approach the girl and talk to her. What could he say and how could he say it? How could he interest her in looking at him? What could he do to impress her?

Then he had a thought. He could write the Declaration of Independence on the chalkboards that filled one whole wall of the room. At least she would have to notice him, maybe ask him what it said, and say something about who she was and where she went to school. Henry didn't really understand longshots and what foolish optimism really was, so he didn't hesitate to put his scheme into action.

He saw that the blackboards had been erased and that nobody had started to write, draw, or scribble anything on them with the abundantly available chalk. Why would they? That was school stuff. As he approached the blackboard, Henry started to repeat to himself the words that he and Larry had memorized. He felt certain that he knew what he was going to write.

Henry found a full, unbroken stick of chalk in the tray and, at first, considered writing in cursive, then stopped and switched to the manuscript, aware that his word formation was better and easier to read with the latter style. He tried to make the words big enough to read from the middle of the room where the girl was sitting but not too big that he would run out of space. He began with, "When in the course of human events it becomes necessary…" then he stopped to make sure necessary was spelled corrctly. He was hoping that he wouldn't make any spelling errors, but before he finished the first paragraph, "impel" came out as "appel" and "separation" as "seperation."

As he started to write, "We hold these truths to be self-evident…," he switched his gaze from the blackboards to where the girl had been sitting and saw that she was no longer there. Had she left? He wondered. He scanned the room and saw that she had moved to a corner where she was staring disconsolately at some small, plastic farm animals. She was not looking at his work at all. Well, maybe she would in a moment, so Henry returned to writing "…that all men are created equal."

By the time he was halfway across the blackboards, he noticed that a couple of younger girls were watching him and pretending to read what he had written. "What is that?" one of them asked.

"It's nothing," he replied. "Just something I'm doing."

A minute or two later, one of the girls picked up the eraser and immediately wiped out some of the first part of the Declaration while the other grabbed a piece of chalk and started writing, "M-A-R-G-A-R-E-T."

"Hey, don't!" Henry looked at them with as stern an expression as he could muster behind his glasses, but they took no notice of him and then Margaret's playmate started writing, "N-A-N-C-Y." He looked out into the room and saw that his girl had still not paid the least attention to his work or what was left of it, so he stopped after writing "Life, Liberty, and the Pursuit of Happiness." What was the use?

Henry walked to the center of the room and considered going out onto the playground to be with Larry, reckoning that his older brother would tolerate his presence as long as he kept his mouth shut. Then a boy walked up to him. "Hi," the boy said. "What was that you were writing on the board?"

The boy looked to be a year or two older, wore long dark brown hair, and was dressed in newer clothes unlike Henry's faded hand-me-downs. But he seemed friendly and intelligent and genuinely curious about the words on the blackboard. "Actually," Henry smiled, "it's the Declaration of Independence."

"Really? Did you memorize it?"

"Yeah, I felt like writing it down, and those little girls erased the first part, so I quit. It goes on, um, 'That — that to, um, secure those rights —'"

"I memorize stuff, too," the boy said. "Listen to this: 'Credo in Deum Patrem omnipotentum, Creatorem caeli et terrae, et in Iesum Christum, Filium, Eius unicum, Dominum nostrum —'"

"What's that?" Henry was genuinely impressed.

"That's the Apostles' Creed. In Latin."

"What's the… Apostles' Creed?

"It's a Catholic thing. Are you Catholic?"

"No, I think I'm a Presbyterian — or maybe a Methodist, I'm not sure."

"I know some people don't like Catholics."

"Lots of my friends are Catholics. My dad says things about Catholics, but I know he voted for the President, and *he's* a Catholic. Anyway, doesn't it say up there, 'All men are created equal?' I mean, the Declaration."

The boy looked over at the board and saw that the words Henry had written to that effect were still there. "Ha! I guess you're right. My name is Glenn. Glenn Monahan. What's yours?"

"Henry Valentine."

"Do they call you 'Harry' or 'Hank?'"

"Sometimes they do, but I don't like it. I'm not sure where 'Hank' comes from. My brother Laurence they call Larry, and sometimes we're 'Larry and Harry,' and I don't like that. A big kid down my street was calling me 'Harry Balls,' and I hated that. I was named after one of my dad's friends."

"Valentine. Do you get stuff from kids for that?"

"At first, but then nobody thinks it's funny after a while."

"Where do you go to school?"

"John Marshall, over on La Palma. I'm in the fourth grade."

"I'm in the sixth. I go to St. Anthony Claret. It's on La Palma too, way down past La Palma Park in East Anaheim. You know where the park is?"

"Yeah. I go there sometimes. They got the stadium. Do you have to wear a uniform to school?"

"Yeah. It's okay. When I become a priest, I'll wear another one."

"You're going to be a priest?"

"Sure. I have an uncle who's a priest and he says that I have the knack for it. He —" Just then, a girl walked up to the boys and interrupted Glenn. It was *the* girl. Up close, Henry thought that she looked prettier than ever, even though she was pouting.

"Gle-enn. What time is it?"

"I don't know," he said curtly. "I don't have a watch."

"When are Mom and Dad going to be done so we can go home? There's nothing to do here."

"Look, Gracie, you got books and toys and games and stuff. Go amuse yourself. Don't bug me."

Gracie gave her brother a mean look, turned to Henry, and gave him the same. Then, she walked to the other side of the room, shaking her head in disgust. "Who's that?" Henry didn't mind the dirty look. At least she looked at him.

"My sister," Glenn said with some disgust in his voice. "Do you have any brothers or sisters?"

"I have three older brothers and two older sisters."

"Really?" Glenn's eyebrows shot up. "Six kids and you're not Catholic?"

Henry wasn't sure what the older boy meant by that, but he wasn't going to inquire. Instead, he asked Glenn if he had any other kids in his family. "No, just Gracie. And she's a stupid slut."

"Hey, listen to this," Glenn said. "'Pater noster, qui es in caelis, sanctificetur nomen tuum, adveniat regnum tuum, fiat voluntas tua, sicut in caelo et in terra.'"

"What's that?"

"The Lord's Prayer in Latin. You know the Lord's Prayer?"

"Yeah. 'Our Father, which art in heaven.' Everybody knows that. Listen, I gotta go find my brother."

Glenn held out his hand. "Well, it was nice meeting you, Henry. Good luck."

Henry shook the boy's hand and smiled. He took one look around the room as he turned away from the older boy and headed toward the door to the playground. Gracie was sitting on a chair with her elbows on her knees and her hands holding up her chin, still wearing that pout he had seen on her face before.

When Henry approached, Larry was standing next to the swing set, talking to one of the sixth graders. "Hey, Henry. Mom just gave me some money and said we could get Cokes out of the machine. Let's go. She said they were almost done, and we can wait by the alley."

On the way home, Henry wondered what a "slut" was and whether it was Latin for little sister.

Breakout
by Bruce Wilson

Nestled in the far reaches of Beverly Hills, a stately building known to locals as "the Last Re-Run," housed an eclectic menagerie of used-up, mostly forgotten character actors and Hollywood hopefuls who'd reached their dotage. Some had been bright television stars in their day, but most of the residents were the faces and voices that never made it past the "Also Appearing" line in the closing credits.

In one wing of the H-shaped complex, at the far end of the hall, a wrinkled old man who was quite the hero to kids growing up six or seven decades ago, snored noisily in a wheelchair parked next to his bed. There was a moth-eaten Navajo blanket draped across his lap, and a signed picture of a white horse hung on the wall above the cowhide headboard. Most of the staff at the Hollywood Siesta Rest Home joked privately that the signature was not truly that of the horse but rather was penned by the masked man holding the bridle.

Without disturbing the old man's nap, Wilbur, the dayshift orderly, wheeled the chair into the sunroom and parked it in a corner away from the game tables and the doily-covered furniture where the female residents liked to hang out. A few of the ladies glanced up as Wilbur rolled the chair past their seats, but quickly returned to the day's subject which was (at least according to Wilbur and his co-workers) always about the soap operas they once starred in. The old man snorted loudly and jerked a little when a second chair was rolled up to the window. He lifted the black silk mask away from his eyes and asked, "Who're you?"

"Who do ya think?" said the new arrival, a once muscular but now flabby man wearing a pointy-eared helmet and a black cape. He pushed the helmet back on his head while a toothless grin spread across his face.

"I hate this place," growled the first man as he pulled the Indian blanket up to his waist.

"Me too. Everything sucks…the food, the service, and the nurses."

The man with the cape was the actor who had played Batman, and at some point in his long career as a crime fighter, he'd *become* the caped crusader. The only clothes he'd brought with him to the rest home were the costumes he'd worn while filming the television program and making public appearances at shopping centers throughout Southern California. When he was young, the tight-fitting jersey, knee-length boots and the bat-like helmet fit him like a glove. But, in time, his once buff body had gone soft and flabby and he'd lost nearly two inches in height. When his hair began to thin and eventually drift away as fluff on his cape or in clumps down the shower drain, the visored helmet became loose and often slipped forward over his eyes.

The grizzled man in the other wheelchair had a long history as well. Though never as muscular as Batman, the Lone Ranger always appeared fit in his all-white (except for the red piping at the shoulders) costume—hat, shirt, pants—riding on his all-white horse, Silver. Like the fella with the cape, the television ranger had long since lost all awareness of his real name and heritage. He had become the Lone Ranger. He quickly replied to Batman's list of complaints.

"Especially the nurses! Those women are scary."

"No kidding," said Batman. "the other day, I was sitting on the side of my bed trying to figure out how to get my cape on, and in walked the head Nazi."

"What'd she do?"

"She started laughing at me and called me 'Bat Guano.' She said I looked like an idiot with a bed sheet for a cape."

The Lone Ranger scratched at the crown of his shiny head and looked across the table set between their chairs. "Sounds like somethin' she'd say. What'd you do?"

Pushing his helmet up above his forehead, he said, "I told her that someday I'd get even with her. But she just laughed and went out to pester someone else."

"God, I hate her."

"Me too." Slowly shaking his head from side to side, he paused, gathering his thoughts. "Anyway, Lone, old buddy, looks like we made it through another day."

"Yep, pardner, another day. How'd you sleep?"

"Okay, I guess. I keep seeing that damned searchlight, though. But I can't tell if it's real or a dream."

"Searchlight?" Lone paused, "the one with the bat?"

Batman shifted in the sling seat of the wheelchair, trying to relieve the pressure on his bony butt. "Yeah, it gives me the creeps…keeps me awake for hours, and then I wake up with very strange feelings."

"Oh god! Here we go again with the feelin's." Over their years together, this topic had popped up frequently and always lead to short, tense moments. "What happened? Did your parents lock you up in the Bat Cave? Did they make you wear dresses or somethin'?"

"Lay off, will you? You're always ragging me about my feelings. You macho Wild West heroes are all alike. Why, just the other day, I was talking with Matt Dillon…" The caped crusader may have been old and forgetful, but he still knew how to get under the skin of his buddy.

"Not him again," said the Ranger, lifting the mask away from his eyes." "I get tired of hearin' about him. He's always braggin' about how good he was with a gun. He used *lead* bullets for cryin' out loud." He absently reached for his gun belt, but it wasn't there. Then, remembering what another famous deputy used to do, he slipped his fingers into his shirt pocket and pulled out a bullet. Holding it between his thumb and forefinger, he thrust it toward Batman.

"I always used silver ones myself."

"Why?" he snickered. "Were you hunting werewolves?"

"Huh? What? No! They were a symbol of…Oh, hell, I forgot what they were a symbol of. But at least they weren't led. Anyway, I never could figure out why Dillon stayed in Dodge City as long as he did. First with that gimp Chester, and then with—who was it—Goober?"

"No, you idiot, Goober was the one in Mayberry with Sheriff Taylor."

Shaking his head wildly, the western star said, "No, he wasn't. Taylor's deputy was Barney Fife. Goober was the one in the Marines."

"Goober? No, it was Gomer who was in the Marines, you knucklehead. Goober was the one on The Love Boat."

Shaking his head again, the Ranger shouted, "There are no boats in Dodge City!"

"Well, whatever, it doesn't really matter. Matt Dillon stayed in Dodge because of Miss Kitty."

"Hell, *I* woulda stayed in Dodge cuz of Miss Kitty."

"Me too," said Batman. "That Miss Kitty was a very hot chick…those long dresses with all of the buttons, man, oh man. And she even had her own saloon."

A dreamy, faraway look crossed the Ranger's face, and he said, "Yeah, a hot woman and a saloon. Women and drinkin', drinkin' and women. Maybe Dillon was smarter than I thought."

Batman seemed to consider the other old man's words and then responded dreamily, "Yeah."

The two didn't speak for a moment, and then the crime-fighter blurted out, "Come to think of it, I've never even been to Dodge City. I spent all of my time in Gotham City. I wasn't even in a western show."

The Lone Ranger chuckled, the giggle sounding much like Silver's stomach after eating bad oats. He looked at his caped friend and said, "Nope, you kept racin' around in your Batmobile with that sissy Robin." He nodded absently and added, "Who names a boy, 'Robin?'"

"Robin wasn't a sissy. He was just…sensitive."

"Like I said, a sissy."

Once again, Batman knew how to shift the negative attention onto the white-suited gentleman. "You should talk. You ran around with an Indian who kept calling you a horse's ass."

"What?"

"Yeah, a horse's ass. What in the hell do you think *Kemosabe* means?"

At once, a confused look spread across the Lone Ranger's face. He lifted his mask and said, "I don't know. I was always afraid to ask. I didn't wanna sound dumb. But Tonto always smiled when he said it. I thought it meant Wise One or He-Who-Talks-Straight or somethin' noble like that."

"Nope," Batman grinned, 'horse's ass.' That's why Tonto was always smiling. I saw it in a Farside Cartoon." With a smile on his own face, Batman asked the Ranger if he'd heard from his faithful Indian companion.

"Well, Tonto ended up a hell of a lot better than us. He's not livin' in the Hollywood Siesta Rest Home, the cesspool of the west."

"Oh yeah, what's he doing these days?"

"He owns a casino in Laughlin, makes millions of bucks every year, eats well, has a big house. He even has grandkids."

"Not bad for an Indian," he said and then added, "makes me hate this place even more."

Nodding his head, the Ranger looked at his long-time friend and said, "No kiddin'. A crappy little room, no company, if you get my drift, only one TV channel, and it don't play nothin' but reruns of Gilligan's Island. God, I hate that show."

Soon enough, Batman's head was nodding in syncopation. "Yeah, and then them Nazi nurses roll us out here into this godawful hot sunroom. These people don't have a clue about our needs."

"Yeah, Batsy, our needs are simple: a soft bed, good food, and a little freedom when we want it."

"That's right, food and freedom. Just like the good old days."

All of a sudden, the Lone Ranger shifted in his seat, becoming antsy as he looked around the room. The hens were still cackling across the room and Wilbur and his white-coated co-workers were out back on the patio taking a smoke break. He whispered as quietly as he could and said, "I've got an idea. I say we break out of here. I say we get some help from some of you old TV buddies and get the hell outta Dodge."

"We're not in Dodge. We're in Beverly Hills."

"I know that you old fool. I mean we gotta get outta *here*, outta this prison."

Finally catching on that the Ranger wasn't kidding, Batman said, "Hey! I've still got the key to the Batmobile…but it may be out of gas, though."

"That's okay," the Ranger said, "Silver always had gas, and that made for an interesting campout for many. Why I remember one time…"

"Not that kind of gas, *Kemosabe.*"

"Oh." A confused look spread over that part of his face below the sagging mask.

"Anyway, who should we call for help?"

"I dunno, Batsy, but whoever we call, we gotta have a plan—a no-fail plan."

Sitting up a little straighter in his wheelchair, Batman pushed his helmet back so he could see Lone. "All right then—let's start with a plan and we'll add help where we need it."

"Well, for sure, it'll have to be at night when the nurses are sleepin'."

"What will have to be at night?"

"The breakout, dummy."

"Oh yeah."

"And we'll have to get someone to push our wheelchairs."

"I don't really need this wheelchair. It's just part of my disguise. You see, when I need…"

"Never mind that," the Lone Ranger said, "you can push me. I *need* my wheelchair."

"Why?"

"That nag, Silver, kept buckin' me off every time I said, 'Let's go big fella!' to her. Anyway, we'll leave at night. You push my chair, then what?"

Getting excited again, Batman said, "We have to blow the lock off of the front door. I saw them do it one time on Mission Impossible. They used some clay stuff, put a fuse in it, and it blew the whole…"

"You dope, we can't blow the lock off; it'll wake everyone up." He was suddenly aware that his raised voice was drawing attention from the ladies in the middle of the room. He reached up to tip his Stetson at them, then remembered he had lost it some time ago. He converted the tip to a wave and gave them a quick wink. One of the ladies harrumphed and turned away, and then the chattering continued. "The noise would probably bring the Nazi runnin' down the hall."

"Oh, yeah. Right. So, we have to pick the lock. How're we gonna do that?"

"I dunno. I guess we'll have to steal the key from the office."

Batman began shaking his head vigorously. "No way, Lone. I'm not going to the office. The last time I went, they did a cavity check on me…said that the reason I keep seeing search lights is because I'm on drugs. They bent me over and… "I've never been so embarrassed."

"I never used any drugs, just peyote," the masked man said proudly.

"Isn't that some kind of a wild dog?"

"No, you fool, those are coyotes. Peyote's a recreational pharmaceutical. Why, me and Tonto used to take a little hit out there under the stars, lay back on our bed rolls and think about the future."

"You got any on you?"

"What? Got any what?"

"Payola, what've we been talking about?"

"Payola? You dummy, it's peyote."

"All right, all right." A bit chagrined, he took a deep breath and said, "Now what were we discussing?"

"Oh, yeah, Miss Kitty," Lone said.

"Yeah, Miss Kitty. We sure never had anyone like her in the Bat Cave."

The Lone Ranger had a dreamy look on his face when he asked, You think she and Dillon ever…you know…?

"Did it? Oh yeah. Lots of times. Every time Dillon went to the saloon, he always sent Chester or Booger off to find the Doc. He and Miss Kitty probably had all kinds of fun up in her room and probably a few quickies behind the bar."

"I never had a quickie. I hardly ever got laid," the Ranger said sadly, straightening his droopy mask. "Hell, even Tonto scored more than I did. I think it was the mask."

"Tonto never wore a mask!"

"*My* mask. The women were afraid of *my* mask. God, you are so dumb."

"Hmmm. Maybe that's why I never got laid. Maybe women didn't like my mask."

"No, the reason you never got laid is that you ran around with a sissy."

"Listen, I told you Robin wasn't a sissy. He just had special needs." Batman looked sad and probably missed having the kid around to tease. "Now, what were we talking about?"

"Uh, oh yeah, goin' to the office to…why were we goin' to the office?"

"To find some coyotes. Then we were gonna…what were we gonna do?"

"I dunno, I forgot." Looking around the room, Lone spotted the television in the corner. "Hey, you wanna watch Gilligan's Island after lunch?"

"Might as well, it's the only thing on television anyway."

"Yeah. These people around here don't really understand our needs."

"Nope. All we need is good food and some freedom."

"Yeah, freedom." The Ranger moved forward in his wheelchair seat and said, "You know what we oughta do?"

"No, what?"

"We oughta break outta here. All we gotta do is…"

"Well…maybe tomorrow."

Standing behind the old men, Wilbur chuckled and said, "Okay, you guys, ready for lunch?"

"Yeah, we're hungry."

The Alchemist
by Chas Wilson

Everything I know about what happened around the Public Library - I used to say to BB that the library was a melting pot of the haves and have-nots, you know, a mixture of homeless people and the rich older folks of the nearby neighborhood. Obviously, it ain't no more. BB said that the one thing that everyone there at the library had in common was that each one, rich or poor, was trying to escape from something in his life. BB used to laugh when I called it a melting pot. He said it was more like a box of rocks. They sort of shake around inside the box and wear each other down, but, in the end, they're still rocks and can't change their basic nature.

BB had names for the different people who came and went to the library. He called the homeless and travelers "plebes." He called the rich old folks "patricians." Everyone else who wasn't a plebe or a patrician he called either "citizens" or "cattle," depending on his mood. Anyway, if BB was right and the library was a box of rocks, well then, BB was a diamond. And if it was a melting pot, then somehow it produced gold.

If I think about it, I guess I've been living here for more than three winters. For me, it hasn't been so bad; it drizzles a lot, but it never gets real cold. A few good tarps will keep you mostly dry. Folks around here are pretty generous to sign-holders like me, so I kind of settled in and don't travel as much as I used to. I work the middle entrance to Target on 23rd Street. I'm actually saving a lot of the money I bring in. I hope to have enough someday to settle down, get a real job, and have a real home. I've been careful with my savings and since I hung out with BB, I felt pretty safe that nobody was going to take it from me. Nobody messed with BB, messed with his stuff, or messed with his friends. I liked to think that I was one of his good friends.

BB was really smart. He always could come up with a good answer for every question I had. But I don't think he had any more schooling than I did, which ain't much. I think he learned everything he knows from books. I think he once said that he was in the circus some years ago and picked up the habit of reading when he was wintered in Florida. He read a lot. In fact, he went into the library every day it was open. Never missed it.

He didn't panhandle. He didn't work. I don't know what he did to get money, but he never seemed to do without food, clothing, or a place to get out of the weather. I sometimes thought he had a sugar mama at the Y, because he went there almost every day and took a shower. I think he must have exercised some, too, because he had bigger muscles than a pit bull.

 The only scrounging that he did was glass jars with lids. He'd take most anyone, as long as it had a screw-on metal lid. You know, like jelly jars, or instant coffee, or pasta sauce. He liked them and called them sacred vessels. He washed them out and filled them with tea, which he called the universal elixir, and drank it during the day. He said he threw the jars away in the library after drinking all the tea. He was kind of funny that way.

The library people didn't seem to worry about him like they did with the rest of us travelers and homeless, I guess, because he was pretty healthy looking and didn't stink. He mostly just wandered around, picked up a book or two, and then settled in one place while he read them. He usually spent an hour or two in the library every day. After he was done with the library, he used to swing by where I was hanging out and ask me if I wanted to go get something to eat and maybe find a jar or two. Then we would take the jar or jars to a fast food restroom to wash them. Any time I'm by myself, they don't usually give me the code for the restroom door. They always gave it to BB.

BB was kind of artistic. Every evening, he used to take this little tool and scratch designs into the glass jars. I asked him once why he wanted to do that if he was just going to throw the jar away the next day. He said it cleaned his spirit to decorate these jars. I didn't know then and don't know exactly what that means now because he used to say that other things he did also cleaned his spirit. Sometimes, he collected rocks and made designs of them in the dirt. To me, the designs looked almost like the streets around the library. BB told me that they were kind of like streets; he called them paths to salvation. Another thing he did to clean his spirit was to go up to the overpass at night, hang by his fingertips, and work his way from one side to the other.

My watch doesn't work sometimes, so I don't know exactly when the fire started at the library. It seems like it was an hour or two after it closed. I had washed up at the Walmart and was walking back from there when I smelled the smoke. As I got closer, I saw the fire climbing up into the sky. There was a woomp every few seconds, and the fire would get taller and brighter. I started to feel it when I was a block away. All the homeless and travelers were standing around and watching the fire. It just kept getting bigger and bigger and kept going, woomp, Woomp, WOOMP! I didn't see BB anywhere. I hoped that he hadn't stayed inside the library or got stuck and couldn't get out. I started walking around and asking everybody if they had seen BB. A couple of people said they saw him near the library in the late afternoon.

The crowd watching the fire kept getting bigger and bigger. Men, women, and children – whole families - were there. I wandered around looking for BB and noticed that hundreds of them were citizens and a whole bunch of patricians had shown up as well. There was a little bit of talk, but mostly everyone just stared at the fire like they were hypnotized. When I asked people if they had seen BB, it was almost like I had to break through an invisible shell to get their attention. It was crazy.

I never could find BB. He just sort of disappeared. There wasn't much more that I could do, so I kind of gave up looking and joined the others watching the fire. It seemed like nobody could move as long as the fire was burning and booming. Once it was put out, people started to wander away. Even though the morning sun was starting to rise, I was dog-tired and wanted to sleep.

When I got to the place where BB and I kept our stuff, I saw that all of his stuff was gone. Someone told me that they heard there had been no bodies in the library. Someone else heard that all the booms that we listened to were made by exploding jars. They said the jars were filled with a mixture of gasoline and motor oil and scarred or scored so they would explode easier. If I didn't know better, I might think that someone re-used all of BB's decorated tea jars. I mean, how else would those jars get into the library?

This afternoon, everyone was talking about how, during the fire, somebody had broken into a whole bunch of the patrician's houses and cleaned out the valuables – cash, jewelry, coins, they even took some pistols and rifles. Most of the patricians didn't find out until they got home from watching the fire. That's about all that I heard, except that it was a big haul. Whoever did it got a bunch of expensive stuff.

I wish BB was still around so he could tell me what he thinks about all this.

(Signed) Stewart Wayne Stultum

No Permanent Address

Henry At The Zoo
by Howard Wilson

Thirteen-year-old Henry was completely worn out, and the summer was almost half over. And it wasn't the summer vacation that was doing it; it was the fact that he was working instead of playing. The only consolation he had from this experience was that he had earned enough money to buy himself something he had wanted for some time — an electric guitar.

Two summers earlier, Henry and his one-year-older brother Larry had been signed up for guitar lessons by their mother. The music store at the Buena Park Shopping Center was offering weekly lessons along with a free classical guitar and an instruction book for only twenty-five dollars each. The lessons would run for six Saturdays straight. Because the Center was within walking distance, it was a way to get the boys interested in something, and active, and out of the house.

The guitars were cheap Japanese imports sold as "the St. George Classique." The book was your standard juvenile, first-level musical instruction quarto with forgettable originals like "Lazy Maisie" and "Down on the Farm," along with old folk tunes like "Long, Long Ago" and "Du Du (Liegst Mir am Herzen)." Since the Beatles had broken out the previous winter, Henry and Larry had wanted a book with something like, "She Loves You." Songs the girls would want to hear. Besides that, the book was for "classical" instruction, so there were no chord charts.

So Larry and Henry spent part of their Saturday afternoons in a class along with a dozen kids and teenagers from nearby neighborhoods, and by the end of the six weeks, Henry, if not Larry, had learned to read music, to tune his guitar, and to play most of the tunes in the book, even "Lazy Maisie." Henry also found that he was able to pick out songs by ear — songs like "And I Love Her" and "Washington Square" — well enough so that others could recognize them. By the end of the summer, brother Larry was done with his guitar, but Henry was ready to take it further.

Henry was aware that the Beatles and the Beach Boys did not play cheap, imported classical acoustic guitars. They played cool electric and, as time went by, that's what Henry wanted. Moreover, Henry imagined that girls liked electric guitars and that Henry had always liked girls. Since starting puberty when he was only ten, Henry's feelings for girls only became more intense.

Henry imagined, with good reason, that the girls were not particularly attracted to him all by himself. He would look in the mirror and see a tall, skinny kid with crooked teeth and goofy goggle glasses. Besides that, he had a weird, deep voice. He dreamed that having an electric guitar and playing in a band would make him attractive to the girls at Brookhurst Junior High.

All the birthdays and Christmases over the next two years failed to produce the instrument that Henry dreamed of. Last Christmas, he was given a small Japanese tape recorder, but when he stuck the recorder's microphone inside the sound hole of his Classique, it did not make it sound like Dick Dale's Fender Stratocaster when he played it back. And then the cheap guitar he had owned for little more than a year and a half had fallen apart altogether. Henry was resigned to the fact that he would have to earn the money to buy an electric with his own money.

So, right after seventh grade, he went to work. Henry's dad's friend Buzzy (his real name was Everett) had married Snickey (her real name was Mavis), a divorcee with three little kids, and because of their financial condition at the time, both Buzzy and Snickey were working full-time. This situation gave Henry the opportunity to earn fifty cents an hour looking after Dick and Dede and Dudley ten hours a day, five days a week.

Three grubby kids and a one-dollar expense account with which to feed them lunch every day was Henry's challenge. Dick was eight and had somehow managed to get promoted from second to third grade without having learned to read. Henry had to sock him in the arm a few times a day to get him to mind. Dede was seven, smart enough, and was allowed to go to her friend's apartment nearby for an hour or two each day, making Henry's job a little easier. Dudley was five and he spent most of his time watching Henry as he read or looked at the TV. Dudley never looked at the TV himself, he just watched Henry. All three kids would accompany Henry to the Colima grocery store to buy the day's provisions, usually sandwich fixings, chips, and Hostess pies. Day in and day out, the weeks passed, and as June turned to July, Henry was done with sandwiches, chips, and Hostess pies.

On Friday of the third week, Henry confided in Larry. "I don't think I can take much more of this. One more week, and I'll have a hundred dollars, enough to buy my guitar."

"Did you tell Dad?"

"Not yet. I'm wondering if you'd want to take over for me."

"Yeah. I guess I could use the money." Somehow, Larry always had money, Henry thought, and he was always looking for ways to get more. "Oh yeah. Cousin Lionel is coming by tomorrow to take me down to

Rancho Bernardo. I'm going to stay the week with Uncle Donald and Aunt Madeleine."

"They invited you? How come they didn't invite me?"

"Dad told them you had a job. Maybe you can go next week?"

So it was settled that Larry would take over Henry's babysitting job starting the next week and that Henry would be a guest of his uncle and aunt after Larry returned. A week's vacation away from home and no more of Snickey's kids — not to mention a new electric guitar. Could things be getting any better?

At the end of his last day, Buzzy handed Henry his twenty-five dollars pay, and his dad agreed to take him to a music store to get his guitar. "Won't you need an amplifier to go with your guitar, son?"

"I guess so. Will a hundred dollars be enough?"

"We'll see what they got. Maybe they'll have some kind of deal."

The music store had Gibsons and Fenders and Rickenbackers, and the salesman was eager to have Henry and his dad buy one of those quality guitars. "You can pay on time and pick it up when you're paid in full." That idea wouldn't work for a boy who wanted to take it home that evening.

"What do you have for a lower budget?" Henry's dad was a car salesman, and he figured that guitars, like automobiles, came in high-end and low-end makes and models. You don't buy a kid a Cadillac for his first car, and neither do you buy a Rickenbacker for his first electric guitar. Henry's dad was looking for his son to buy himself a guitar that would be equivalent to a Rambler.

So the salesman led them to an opposite wall where the store displayed fancy-looking electric models, and Henry pointed to a red guitar that looked boss. It had one pickup and a cutaway, and the price tag said, "Harmony Stratotone — $74.99."

"Can I try this one?" Henry picked it up, and the pleasure he felt from holding a real electric guitar was evident to both his dad and the salesman. The salesman grabbed a cable and plugged the guitar into a demo amp.

"Have a seat on this stool and play us something," the salesman said as he switched on the amplifier. Henry had not played a guitar since the top of his Classique scrolled up six months earlier, so he was a bit rusty when he played "Louie Louie" and then stopped to make some adjustments to the tuning. "Sounds good!" the salesman said with practiced enthusiasm. "Now you'll need an amplifier." The salesman showed them a line of Marshalls and Fenders in the range of prices way beyond Henry's means. Then he led Henry and his dad down to the small practice amps, but none of them cost less than a hundred bucks.

"Don't you have anything less than that?" Dad was certain that he could get everything his boy needed without spending more than what Henry had in his wallet. "Any returns or shopworn merchandise?" This is where the old man's car sales experience went to work. "I know Sears has stuff like that sometimes."

The salesman went into his "let me think" routine and then walked to the back of the store and a few minutes later returned carrying a small ten by ten black box with a dusty tweed speaker cover and a couple of dials on the face. "I know this one works, but let me demonstrate it to you." He plugged it into the power outlet, inserted the cable, and played a blues lick on the Stratotone. "I can let you have it for thirty dollars." It wasn't too loud, but Henry could hear the possibilities in the midget amp.

Dad was determined to leave Henry with some change left over. To the salesman: "How about we take the amp off your hands? Eighty-five for the amp and guitar." He looked at his son. "I'll make up the tax for you, Henry."

"Let me check with the manager." Henry's dad knew what that meant. The salesman was ready to deal and name a slightly higher price, but he did not want to make it look like he was giving in too easily. He came back in a couple of minutes. "I can go ninety." So the deal was made: his dad paid the four-fifty tax, and Henry had his gleaming red Harmony Stratotone, pigmy practice amp with cable, and a few picks. He could not wait to get home and fire it up.

The previous Christmas, Henry's eldest brother Brad had given him a guitar strap — real bonded leather — and now he could use it. Since he hadn't played guitar in several months, he no longer had the calluses on the tips of his fingers, and even those had developed from playing the softer nylon strings of his classical guitar. The new electric had steel strings. Besides that, the action was set a little high, and after playing for a few minutes, Henry's pads were sore. It was somewhat discouraging, but the thrill of owning an electric guitar overrode the slight disappointment, and he vowed to practice every day.

Strapped to his Harmony Stratotone, Henry stood before the full-length mirror on the door in his bedroom and tried to imagine how he would look to the girls at Brookhurst Junior High. He switched on the amp, turned the volume dial all the way to the right, and strummed over and over the coolest chord he knew, D7. Henry tried to look boss. Wouldn't it be great if he could get a band together? His friend Dave had a drum set, and many guys also had guitars.

"Turn it down!" His dad called from across the hall. "You don't need it that loud just to practice." Henry was glad that he could get enough sound from the little practice amp to be heard outside his bedroom. Maybe it would be loud enough to play at school dances with his band.

The next day, Cousin Lionel brought Larry back from Rancho Bernardo, and it was Henry's turn to visit. Lionel was nineteen, tall and athletic, affable, and reasonably intelligent, but a little wild, so as much as Henry liked him, he was also a little afraid of him. "We want to see your guitar," Lionel said as soon as he and Larry came into the house. So, Henry led them back to the bedroom that he shared with his brother and displayed his Stratotone with pride.

Lionel said, "Okay, Henry, play it for us. Play it loud."

"My dad told me not to play it loud."

"Uncle Stan won't mind as long as I'm here and he isn't. Go ahead."

So Henry strummed a few D7s at full blast, then turned it halfway down and played "Penetration," a surf tune, one note at a time. "That's pretty good," Lionel said. "Keep practicing." Henry switched it off and started getting ready for his trip south.

After packing his suitcase, Henry carried it with his guitar and amp into the living room. "You're not taking that to your uncle's house," his mom said.

"But, Mom, I gotta practice."

"You can practice when you get home. Put those things back in your bedroom before you leave. And have a good time."

Larry had gone right out after he came home so Henry had little idea of what his visit would be like. Lionel and he chatted on the way down, mostly about music and baseball. The California Angels American League baseball team had just started its first season in Anaheim after five years in Los Angeles. "Why does Anaheim have a big-league ball club and San Diego doesn't?" Lionel griped. "San Diego is a lot bigger and all we have is the Coast League Padres." Whenever Lionel got excited about something, he would start driving faster. When the discussion turned to baseball, Henry noticed that the speedometer needle was just under ninety miles an hour. Henry nervously suggested they change the subject. He was glad to get to Rancho Bernardo without serious injury.

Aunt Madeleine, who was a librarian at San Diego State College during the school year, welcomed Henry into her home, explaining that Uncle Donald would be arriving later. Henry wasn't disappointed. He knew that Uncle Don was partially responsible for Lionel's inferiority complex; his nickname for his son was "Big Dummy." As bad as Henry's dad could be sometimes, he was glad that his uncle was just his uncle. Aunt Madeleine was Lionel's stepmother and, for her part, she treated the big guy, as far as Henry could tell, with kindness.

And his aunt was nice to Henry. He could tell by some of the things she said that she was making favorable comparisons between him and his brother Larry. Henry knew that Larry gave the impression to some people of being conceited and overbearing until they got to know him better. Lionel left on a date or something so Aunt Madeleine and Henry ate supper after which she fluffed up a genuine down comforter so that the boy could sleep comfortably on the sofa. He was allowed to lie on the couch and watch an old movie on television, something with Joseph Cotten, but he fell asleep almost immediately.

The next morning, Aunt Madeleine fixed eggs benedict with fresh-squeezed orange juice and an English muffin with home-canned strawberry jam they bought from a roadside stand. Henry thought, Man, this is living. He could do that for a week. In fact, that was a special breakfast, but he was permitted to fix his own for the rest of his stay, and he did so without complaining, even to himself.

Knowing that Henry was a reader, his aunt let him into her personal library which filled one of the spare rooms. Some classic works of literature were on the shelves, some he knew of, and others he did not. He pulled out a leather-bound edition of *David Copperfield* and opened it to the title page.

"Good choice," Aunt Madeleine said and turned to leave the room. "Let me know if you have any questions." There was a comfortable-looking chair in the library next to a small side table, so Henry sat down and began reading, getting through the first five paragraphs before giving in to the urge to see what other treasures the library held.

Eventually, Henry found a whole shelf of art books, each slim volume featuring the works of a great painter. He opened one up and saw a picture he had always loved, one that had decorated a record album box of light classical music his parents owned. "Le Moulin de la Galette," it was captioned. He turned a few pages and saw another painting that stimulated him in more ways than one. It was captioned, "The Bathers." Henry looked at the cover and saw that the artist's name was Renoir. "Ren-oyer," he said to himself. There were other books in the series, featuring painters from every era but the ones he liked were Cezanne, Gaugin, Monet, Van Gogh (he knew about him), and particularly this guy whose name was Modigliani.

Something told Henry that their names, being foreign, might not be pronounced "Ren-oyer" or "Gowj-in" or "Moan-ett," so he looked at the text at the beginning of each book and, sure enough, everyone had a pronunciation key, and he was able to commit the right pronunciations to memory. Throughout the week, Henry looked at every painting in the books of the painters that he admired, and, at one point, his aunt came in. "You like the Impressionists?" she asked.

When Henry looked at her quizzically, Aunt Madeleine said, "Those painters, Renoir and Cezanne and the others, they're called Impressionists except Modigliani. I'm glad you like them. It shows you have mature tastes." Henry didn't mention that he also had a taste for paintings of nude women.

The week drifted by; Henry studied his aunt's art books, read a chapter or two of Dickens, walked in the woods behind their house, and watched old movies with his aunt and uncle. Uncle Donald was back and forth from work as a sales representative, so Henry didn't see as much of him as he expected, but he enjoyed his company because his uncle seemed to be amused by Henry's quips and observations.

On Friday, Lionel came by as previously planned to take Henry to the San Diego Zoo. What he didn't expect was that Lionel was bringing a couple of other kids with him, and Henry was a little putout, not wanting to be crowded by a couple of kids he didn't know, besides having to behave more formally as is always the case when being involved with strangers. But they seemed to be nice kids.

Eric was a little more than a year older than Henry, while his sister Julie was a couple of months younger, having just turned thirteen in June. The boy was maybe an inch shorter than Henry's five-foot-ten but was strongly built, had a good sense of humor, and turned out to be energetic. He even laughed when Lionel's freeway speed tickled a hundred miles per hour. He knew baseball and was a fan of the Los Angeles Dodgers.

In Henry's eyes, sister Julie was just plain beautiful. She was about five-foot-three with short, honey-colored hair and a few freckles splashed across her nose. Her eyes were a medium blue, and her nose was straight and symmetrical. When she smiled, she showed even teeth behind her lips which were adorned with pale pink gloss. Julie was slender but not waiflike and was showing hints of adolescent development that Henry found impossible to ignore.

Julie sat in the front passenger's seat while Eric and Henry talked baseball in the back. "Why do you like the Angels when they've never won anything?"

"They're my home team. I'm from Anaheim, and they play at Anaheim Stadium."

"That makes sense. San Diego needs a big-league team. I don't care much for the Padres." Eric looked from the window to Henry. "So, who's your favorite player? Mine's Don Drysdale."

"Not Koufax? Mine's Jim Fregosi."

"Nah. Koufax is a lefty. Fregosi's good. Good fielder, and he can hit."

The conversation continued like this for a while, and then Lionel started talking about a new movie he wanted to see called *The Wild Angels*.

"It's about the Hell's Angels and I hear it's pretty good." By the time they reached the zoo, they had nearly exhausted the subject of cool movies, although Julie had little to say about them.

The four of them made their way into the reptile house and, past the stinking flamingos, saw the big cats, bears, and monkeys and apes of all kinds. Julie did not quite ignore Henry but stayed aloof until Eric's teasing of her became tiresome. Then she started talking more and more to Henry, asking him what his favorite school subjects were.

"I like geography and English. I like to read."

"Yeah, me too. What books do you like?"

"I'm reading *David Copperfield* right now," Henry said, making up his next reading project on the spot, "and probably *Moby Dick* next. What's your favorite?"

"Book or subject?"

"Subject."

"Art. I love art. I want to be a painter."

"I love art too. I really like the Impressionists."

Julie suddenly became animated, stopped, and turned towards Henry, pressing her palms together. "Really? Me too! I love them. Who's your favorite painter?"

Henry was glad that he remembered how to pronounce their names. "Renoir. He's always been my favorite. I like Seurat too — and Monet."

"Oh, I love Monet." Julie was making eye contact now and Henry was conscious of nothing but how beautiful she was and how grateful he was to have discovered those books in Aunt Madeleine's library. He had seen enough caged animals to last him the rest of the day, but with her passion for paintings, this creature by his side had all his attention.

"What are you guys doing back there?" Eric noticed that his sister and Henry were several paces behind them and not looking up at the hyena on the hill. "Lionel says we're going to the lunch stand now."

During lunch, nothing was said about anything in particular. Henry was contemplating buying Julie a souvenir with some of the ten dollars he had left after buying his guitar. His guitar!

"Julie, do you like music?"

"What kind of music?"

"Any kind. You know, Beatles, Rolling Stones, Lovin' Spoonful?"

"Yeah, I like all that. I got a guitar for my birthday but don't know how to play it yet."

"I play guitar. I've been playing for years and I just bought myself an electric guitar. I wanted to bring it down with me but I couldn't." Then Julie smiled her biggest smile at Henry, and it was like a jolt. He forgot what he looked like and where he was and what time it was. Everything at that point was Julie. He wanted to hold her hand for one last walk around the zoo, but it never happened. Lionel told the three teenagers to wait near the bust of the gorilla Ngagi while he brought the car around from the parking lot.

Henry thought that maybe he could sit in the back seat with Julie and let Eric ride a shotgun on the return trip to Rancho Bernardo. Maybe they could talk more about art and music — anything but baseball. Maybe he could get her address and write to her. Maybe.

Then, *whoosh*! A tourist with a sixteen-ounce cup of ice-cold Coca-Cola walked past; looking back at some site and not watching where he was going, he stumbled into Julie and poured the whole cup of soda down her back. Henry saw it happen and froze. Eric burst out laughing, and Lionel ran up to her and asked her if she was okay. The tourist apologized over and over and ran to get some napkins to let her wipe herself off. "Everybody, just leave me *alone!*" She screamed the last word and Henry saw his dream of romance evaporate in the sun the way the Coke was evaporating on the pavement near Ngagi.

There was never another word from Julie all the way back to Rancho Bernardo. She sulked in the front seat and did not respond to Lionel's assurance that she would be okay getting dry clothes when she got home. Henry was reduced to talking baseball with Eric in the back seat. When Lionel dropped the pair off, Henry knew he would never see Julie again.

But he was still in love with her and the first night back in Anaheim, he dreamed that Julie was going to marry Don Drysdale and he was intensely jealous.

Sometimes Rabbits Die
by Bruce Wilson

The sad looking face of the young Cub Scout peered out of the fading black-and-white photograph. His shabby, make-shift uniform, the scuffed oxfords he was wearing, and the cluttered porch on which he stood, all seemed to match his mood. Seeing this picture of myself again, after so many years, filled me with a familiar loneliness. I remembered that we couldn't afford a new uniform, so my parents bought me a used shirt and cap. I even had to borrow the Cub Scout manual in order to work on merit badge projects. Even now, I don't recall events so much as I remember feelings, and sights, and fears, and that on the day the picture was taken I learned a lot about the fragility of childhood—a lesson that I've never forgotten. Isn't it strange how sometimes a picture reveals more than it shows?

Growing up in Southern California in the fifties should have been idyllic, and, in many ways, it was. Kids who grew up on farms had wide-open fields and tick-filled woods for their adventures; city kids had their narrow alleys and trashy vacant lots. We had the canyon. The desert east of San Diego started just down the street from our front door. In the canyon, we could hike, hunt, and play surrounded by cactus and mesquite. We could run for hours down sandy arroyos and climb all day on avalanching dunes. With our pinewood swords and Red Ryder BB guns, we fought enemies both imagined and real—like the older kids at school who razzed us about being scouts. Regular treks in the canyon allowed us to study the habits of rattlesnakes, horny toads, and trap-door spiders. Keeping our eyes and ears tuned to the things we saw helped us to discover truths about life that would mean more when we were older. But in 1954, the truths were still mysteries.

As I remember it, one hot Saturday that summer, when my mom was our leader, our Cub Scout den took a hike. Even though we were hoping to earn a merit badge, we hadn't done much planning. But, when the morning of the big day arrived, we were ready to venture out into the canyon. With an adult in charge, we knew we could hike well beyond our usual limits. We only planned on being gone for a few hours, so we just took a couple of canteens of water and some oranges—"fruit for the hand" my mom used to call it. We gathered our gear, lined up in no particular order, and headed south down the two blocks to the end of the street which overlooked the canyon. The sun had just come up tour left an hour before and the fog over the ocean ten miles to our right was glowing pink. The sky was blue, the air was fresh, and summer vacation was just getting started. What an adventure! As our troop of a dozen eight-year-olds and a nearly-thirty mother of six stepped off of the concrete onto the sandy trail, we had no idea what we would experience that day.

The hundreds of look-alike tract homes of our subdivision were built on a mesa, so our primary direction was down as well as south. The trail wound around boulders and scattered stands of prickly pear cactus as it made its way to the floor of the canyon. This was the easy part of the trip. It was still cool and as we walked in the long, blue-gray shadow of the mesa, our energetic eight-year-old bodies weren't even close to being tired. Even this early in the hike, some of the kids were fifty yards ahead of my mom, who was gingerly choosing her steps in order to avoid the cactus spines that lined the side of the trail.

At the foot of the mesa was a twisted mini-forest of green-leafed, re-branched manzanita. Nurtured by a little stream of gutter run-off from the lawn-watering and car-washing of the subdivision above, the heavy-duty shrubs seemed, at first, much grander than the two tall castor trees that stood off to one side. The small fruit we saw hanging from most of the tree branches was, to us, the perfect ammunition for slingshots and throwing. But on this day, not one of us ventured anywhere near the trees.

A few weeks earlier, when the trees had begun to bear their enticing fruit, a tragedy had occurred in our neighborhood. A bunch of us had been playing football in the street. In front of our house when we heard the wailing siren of a fire truck or ambulance. The sound was coming from the main road and seemed to be heading into our neighborhood. For a moment, the action of our game stalled as we tried to determine where the siren was going. The sound grew and then stopped just one block over. We tossed the mini-sized rubber football we'd been using onto our porch and took off running. It wasn't often that we had an opportunity to see police cars or fire trucks, so football quickly lost its allure.

As we rounded the corner, we could see a police car and an ambulance parked crookedly in front of the third house from the end. A crowd had started to gather as we ran toward the flashing lights. Unlike big cities, there weren't enough people in our neighborhood to create a mob, but the crowd of adults and kids looked mob-sized to us. In the back of the ambulance were two small, cloth covered bodies. We pushed our way through the crowd to get closer to the ambulance. We'd never seen dead bodies close-up, and, unfortunately for us, the two policemen made sure we wouldn't on this day. The adults were whispering a lot, casting quick glances at the weeping mother of the two boys. They said it was castor beans that killed the two kids that day. Later that night, ever kid in the neighborhood heard the same story from his folks. "Castor beans are poisonous. Don't touch 'em. Don't even go near those trees or you'll end up like those two poor kids on Encinitas Avenue."

So we gave the trees a wide berth as we passed them. It was almost as if they were haunted. We knew that they were the cause of some kids dying, so they seemed to take on a monstrous look. Even though the trees looked like giant house plants, to us their thin branches looked like monster's arms and we were convinced that their palm-like leaves were clawed hands. I seem to recall that, even though the air was beginning to warm, I shuddered as a trickle of sweat ran down my back.

Once the trail turned away from the trees and the surrounding manzanita bushes, we quickly forgot the danger and got around to the real business of our hike. Pretty soon we were tossing stones and oranges at the tall cactus and the occasional lizard caught sunning itself on the rocks. We watched a hawk circling in the clear sky and imagined buzzards searching for dead bodies in a smoldering wagon train. With our imaginations operating at full speed, we thought we could be ambushed by Apaches in the rocks ahead lust like in the movies. We captured a few small horny-toads and tormented them until they spit blood out of their eyes. (Hey, legends are very hard to discredit when you're eight.) Of course, all of that physical activity generated gigantic thirst. Although we didn't pay much attention to it at the time, our canteens were soon empty and the oranges, at least those that hadn't been tossed at cactus to see if they would stick on the spines, were quickly consumed. We were just having too much fun.

Up ahead, one of the kids started yelling as if he'd discovered buried Mexican treasure, so we forgot whatever it was we were doing and sped down the trail to see what he'd discovered. As we caught up to him, we saw that just off the edge of the path, partially covered by some broad cactus leaves, was a dead rabbit. It looked as if it had been caught by a coyote or bobcat, because its belly had been ripped open. We all acted as if the sight and the awful dead-rabbit smell didn't upset us. However, looking at the rabbit's guts, with dozens of maggots crossing the iridescent visceral landscape like nomads on a trek, the oatmeal I'd had for breakfast began churning in my stomach. My mom hold us to leave the dead bunny alone and hurry up, because she "wasn't gonna give any merit badges to boys who did nasty things."

For the next hour or so we kept wandering south. We were easily distracted by the things we found—a glittery rock we were certain was gold, a disorderly pile of bones that probably belonged to a cousin of the jackrabbit we'd seen earlier, and lots of other neat stuff. No one brought along a compass, and my mom had no sense of direction (at least that's what my dad had said on one of our many trips to see my uncle in Arizona), so we had no idea that we were lost.

As we came over the crest of a ridge, we looked down on a long, silver-colored pipe that served as a bridge over a deep arroyo. The pipe looked big enough to roll a basketball through (if we'd had a basketball to roll) and it had a flat walking surface on top with a handrail on one side. Across the arroyo was a ranch house—you know the kind, made of raw-cut boards, with a covered porch along the whole front of the building, and a rock chimney on one end. We could tell it was a ranch because it looked like those in the cowboy movies we usually saw at the picture show. The only thing missing, it seemed to us, were corrals full of horses. We hoped there was somebody home who would give us a drink of water and let us fill our canteens.

We ran down the slope of the ridge and ventured out onto the pipe. Most of the boys weren't afraid of heights, so barely touching the handrail, they ran across to the other side. Some of us, though, were afraid. Once we were on the pipe (which by now had shrunk to the thickness of a pencil) and had grabbed the thread-like handrail, some of the kids looked down into the deepest gulch they'd ever seen and swore that they could see China at the bottom. I don't know what was at the bottom, because I didn't look. The trip across for those of us afraid of heights was much slower and caused gallons of sweat to pool in the palms of our hands, making our already tenuous grips on the rail that much worse.

We barely had time to catch our breath when we saw an angry looking guy with a shotgun running out of the ranch house in our direction. He was screaming in a mixture of English and Spanish and we thought we heard him yelling something about chickens. Even though we knew we were dying of thirst, not one of us felt like stopping to ask him for a drink of water as he high-tailed it back to the bridge. The shotgun had by that time become as large as a cannon and each of us was sure that we were going to be blasted with pellets. Our thirst and fear of the gulch disappeared as we quickly crossed the arroyo on the bridge that now seemed as wide as a highway.

Bumping and jostling to be in front, we ran for at least five minutes. I kept looking back to make sure my mom was still with us because it wouldn't do for a scout to lose his mom in the wilderness—they don't give merit badges for that. We were running out of breath and had begun to slow down when the trail suddenly ended at a chain link fence. Some of the kids just flopped onto the sand, others simply bent over as if to puke. But each of us was gasping desperately to take some much-needed air into our burning lungs. We were also extremely thirsty, so we started checking the canteens for water again. Our cotton-thick tongues needed relief quickly, but the war-surplus aluminum canteens were even dryer than our mouths. As my mom staggered up to the fence, she told us to get out our oranges because the juice would surely satisfy us. We had to confess that we'd already eaten them, but the smell of the orange juice on our dirty hands reminded us of how we'd wasted them. My mom may not have seen the guilt on our faces, but we did, and not one of us would confess to throwing the oranges at the cactus earlier that day.

In the hour or so that we stayed by the fence, we should have rested and conserved our energy, but, even as exhausted as we were, we couldn't sit still or stay quiet. From the start, nearly everyone was talking at the same time: "What're we gonna do? I'm thirsty! We're lost, aren't we? I wish my dad was here. I should've brought a compass." We were so caught up in our panic that we couldn't come up with a plan. My mom finally told us to be quiet and to rest. She said she needed to think, and she couldn't do it if we kept yelling.

I remember sitting on the ground with my back to the fence. I had closed my eyes and started thinking about what had happened that morning. It was in those hot, quiet moments that I really felt lost; not just lost in the desert, but some deeper feeling of loss. Somehow, my eight-year-old brain made a connection between the dead rabbit and my dead neighbors. I *knew* about death, but only in very simple terms. My mom's father had died a year earlier; I knew that's what happened to old people. His death had little meaning for me, because he lived far away, and I had only been with him once or twice. I had seen dead dogs and cats before, and once I had even caught my little brother choking a baby duck. But the death of two kids I had seen in the neighborhood and at school was unsettling. Children weren't supposed to die. I they could die, I thought, couldn't I? What made me think that I could be indestructible? Getting lost in the desert was one thing, thinking about death was clearly another. Somehow, I recognized that, even though I was still a kid, I had become a little older, a little different. I may not have been able to explain it at the time—few eight-year-olds could have—but I remember feeling that some of my childhood disappeared that day.

Then, my mom suddenly stood up, brushed the sand off of the seat of her pants, put her hands on her hips and took charge. "We're going back to the chicken ranch," she said. "They'll have water and a telephone. We'll call your dad and he'll come get us." Apparently, during the few moments of quiet, her brooding instincts had kicked in. She may have been lost, she may even have been afraid, but she had definitely become determined. She wouldn't listen to any of our arguments about the man who had yelled at us or about his huge shotgun. She had decided what we would do. We stood (somewhat fearfully I remember), made sure we had all of our stuff, and turned to head back down the trail toward the arroyo and the ranch and the shotgun.

We had taken only a few steps when we heard the sound of a car or truck coming along the fence from the opposite direction of the ranch. We all turned and started cheering in our youthful, though somewhat dry voices. Roaring like a bull and sending up great clouds of dust and sand, the dark green Border Patrol panel truck slid to a stop in front of us. All of a sudden our glee turned to fear; we knew we were in trouble now. We'd heard the stories about how the patrol would lock kids up in old prison cells (made out of sandstone like the ones I'd seen at the Yuma Territorial Prison the year before), until they confessed to every crime since Cain killed Abel. The arrival of the truck did nothing to dispel those myths.

It's interesting how most of the time an eight-year-old boy wouldn't want his mom around, but that was one day when I was glad she was with me. She explained to the agents what had happened and they put us kids in the rear of the truck for our ride back home. According to them we'd wandered into Mexico at the ranch and were lucky that we weren't in a Mexican jail. My mom sat between the two Border Patrol agents chattering like a monkey as she filled them in on the details of our adventure. We, however, sweated in the back of the truck. Every one of the dozen of us crammed into that caged enclosure was absolutely quiet. This change in our attitudes—from the exuberant yelling at the start of the hike to the present somber quietude—was, I think, largely due to fear. What would happen to us? Would we be put in jail? Would we get kicked out of Cub Scouts for violating an international border? Would we have to stay in the hot box of the panel truck forever? We sweated, of course, but this sweat had the odor of fear in it.

Now, more than sixty years later, the canyon is a large county park with trees and lawns and tables for family picnics. Mexico is still the same distance south of the old neighborhood, but a steel wall prevents undocumented immigrants from entering the United States and Cub Scouts from getting lost in a foreign country. I grew up a lot that summer day in 1954. Even though I couldn't have expressed it at the time, I think I knew, albeit at a primal level, that life is fragile. Yet, today, I'm convinced that what I learned then, even enhanced by half a lifetime of experiences, is still valid. Even now, looking at the old photograph, I understand why I looked so sad, so lost. I can still feel the sweat, smell the oranges, see the inside of that jackrabbit, and hear the siren of the ambulance as it carried away the bodies of the two kids. And I remember that death, however natural, isn't pretty and it's the same for rabbits and little boys.

If I Could Speak Italian
by Chas Wilson

Susan and I had to run to catch the regional train. It had been raining rather hard all day and inside the terminal it was still quite wet despite being under cover. We juggled our shopping bags and umbrellas and slipped and slid into the first open car and then darted into a sparsely occupied compartment. We collapsed on the bench seat prattling and giggling. Not much of a journey ahead. Three stops. We'd be in Vicenza in less than two hours.

There was only one other person in the compartment, a bloke in a sort of wearied sprawl on the opposite bench. He looked as if most of the rain fell only on him. His black hair was dripping and his linen jacket and jeans were soaked. His head was down when we slid the door closed but he raised it when we scampered in. He smiled at us and dropped his head back down. God, but he was deadly gorgeous!

My mum's Italian and most of her family lives in Veneto. It was Mum's idea for Susan and me to spend our summer holiday here. It was her gift for my high school graduation (Out the door in '84!). It's worked out quite well, really. My aunts and cousins make certain we depart each morning with a generous lunch bundle, so that allows us extra to spend on ourselves. It's terrific! We haven't ended a day out of money.

Much to Mum's dismay and mine now, I never learned Italian. Susan learned Spanish at high school and twists it enough to make herself understood by many of the locals. Me, I struggle enough with the Queen's English! If I could speak Italian, I'd say something to that fella across from us. I don't know, perhaps I would tell him that merely looking at him makes me weak in the knees. Dream on, Jennifer, his ears might as well be painted on!

Over an hour passed and the Sphinx hadn't moved or spoken. Susan and I talked about everything and nothing, nibbling on licorice biscuits and sipping soft drinks. As we got closer to Vicenza, we began chatting about films and music. That's it! I remembered who our compartment mate resembled.

"Look at him, Susan. He looks just like that fella that sings, 'I'm never gonna dance again.' George, George…"

"Maybe you mean George Michael of Wham," he said. "The song is Careless Whisper."

"You're a bleeding Yank and speak English! Why didn't you say something?"

"I just did."

I was all over him after that. I interrogated him with nonstop questioning and he seemed unaffected, almost as if he had been through this many times before. I learned that he was James, an American from Nebraska, a "JG" in the navy, here in Vicenza on temporary duty with his captain, and leaving for sea duty in two days. Susan was visibly shocked when we pulled into Vicenza and I asked him to dinner. I'm not sure what we would have done if he had said yes. I was more shocked when he said that he already had plans for dinner at an Army major's home near Caserma Ederle, but that he was sure that I could come along, if I liked. We agreed to meet in front of the train station in a little more than an hour. He jumped up and said, "See you in a bit," and dashed out of the compartment.

"Jenn! You're bloody mad, you know," Susan scolded, "You're in a foreign country, meeting a strange man who must be at least five years older than you, and going God knows where with him! To top it off, you're having dinner with more strangers, you need a bath, and the only nice clothes you have are snap, crackle, and pop!"

My aunt was beside herself when I walked out of her front door. My hair is fiery red and shaved clean on the left side. I had just washed it and let the rest go where it chose to go. I wanted to look my best for James so I had on a green bustier, a purple crinoline skirt (I made it myself), green fishnet stockings, black lace-up boots, purple fingerless gloves, tons of purple and green beads and bracelets, and one green and one purple hoop earring. Oh yes, and green eye shadow. Oh auntie dear, girls just want to have fun! I arrived a few minutes early and had to suffer the whistles of the dingoes at the train station.

James arrived precisely on time. He stepped out of the cab and kept the door opened for me. He was wearing black trousers, black shoes, a French-blue shirt, open at the neck, and a black leather sport coat. As I slid into the rear seat, he said, "You look nice." He looked nice as well and…smelled terrific!

He told me in the cab that we were going to Robert and Karen Johnson's home. James had also visited there the previous night. He said they were childless and enjoyed company. I worried out loud that I had never known any military people and wasn't certain how to act. "Just be yourself," he suggested, "It'll be fun."

Major "Just call me Bob" Johnson was about thirty, short, very trim, and energetic. He nearly broke my bones with his handshake. Karen was quite a bit younger, twenty-five perhaps, and seemed a little anxious. She looked at James and then at me and it almost seemed as if she were sizing me up. Odd. I reckon I was seen as no threat because she immediately switched to warm and welcoming. She was cute with short hair and perfect teeth. She busied herself in the kitchen while Bob fixed drinks in the lounge room. Dinner was served in the dining area a few moments later. The meal was little different than what my aunts served – pasta, meat, salad, fruit, mineral water, and red wine.

What was different was the conversation; Bob and I couldn't agree on anything! Every time I opened my mouth he was contradicting me. Not one to take that lying down, I began to do the same to him. Then James performed the smoothest magic act. I wish I could say how he did it, but somehow he questioned and spoke to each of us in such a way that not only was I no longer upset with Bob, I was actually starting to see his point of view. I could see that James was doing the same with Bob, who he consistently addressed as "Sir."' My, was he polished. Karen noticed too. She absolutely beamed at him. After dinner we went into the lounge room for dessert and drinks.

Bob said that since coming to Italy, he had become devoted to opera. Bloody hell if James couldn't discuss it with him! They discussed who was better, Verdi or Puccini, as if they were sport stars. James even dug into Bob's record collection and pulled out something by Bizet. While it was playing, they both sat listening, moving their hands like conductors, and giving each other knowing nods. I thought I saw James wink at Karen while this was going on, but I wasn't sure.

Karen brought in some port and chocolate. The talkfest continued. There wasn't a subject that anyone brought up that James couldn't intelligently discuss, yet somehow he made each of us feel more knowledgeable than he was. I don't know about the others, but he certainly made me feel special. Bob was grinning at him. Karen was gazing warmly. But I was feeling something else, almost like make-believe. Is this real?

Bob graciously thanked me for coming and said that he had to go to bed. He had to be at physical training early in the morning. He stifled a yawn, thanked James for coming and for bringing me, and left for bed. Karen asked if either of us wanted coffee and we both declined. Then she put on a Frank Sinatra album and sat down on the opposite end of the sofa from James. Conversation tapered and each of us settled into a dreamy state. I was listening to Sinatra and watching James and Karen. They were looking intently at each other.

When the album finished, James got up and turned it over. When he sat down, he had moved to the middle of the sofa. A few songs later, Karen rose and refilled our glasses. When she returned to the sofa, she had moved into the space that had been between them. I was starting to feel invisible and hypnotized by the unfolding scene. Having to go to the loo forces clarity. I interrupted the reverie and asked where the toilet was.

When I returned, James was singing, "When I was twenty-one, it was a very good year..." and leaning across Karen while taking her glass from her hand. Jesus, Mary, and Joseph, I'm right here but might as well be invisible and Bob's just down the hall!

"I need to go home. Karen, can I call a cab?"

"No need, I'll give you a ride."

So it was quickly arranged that Karen would give me a ride home. I was to ride up front with Karen, to give her directions, while James sat in the back seat. At the last moment I jumped into the back seat with James and we started off. I leaned over the seat next to Karen and guided her.

When we were a short distance from my aunt's house, I turned and pounced on James, wrapped my arms around him, and gave him a kiss to rival any I'd ever seen in films. I kept his arms pinned and stayed locked on until we pulled to a stop, then I said breathlessly and loudly enough for Karen to hear, "Meet me in front of the train station tomorrow morning at nine." James coughed out an "okay" and then I leaped out. I'm almost certain I heard Karen say, "Thanks a lot, James."

As I was doing my nightly routine before going to bed I looked in the mirror, thinking about the day and wondering if I will get up to meet him at the train station.

"Not bloody likely," I said out loud.

Henry's Bid for High Office
by Howard Wilson

Ninth-Grade Presidential Candidates (L-R): Sylvia Shepard, Henry Valentine

Fourteen-year-old Henry greatly admired his fifteen-year-old brother Larry, who was Student Body president at Brookhurst Junior High School. Five years earlier, the boys' older brother Jack had been in the same distinguished office, and as the school year was winding down, it occurred to Henry that he may try the election game himself.

It seemed to some that Henry was looking to fail. Comparisons to Larry were not kind comparisons. Whereas Larry was good-looking, charming, and charismatic, Henry was a tall, skinny, bespectacled, well-read kid with pimples, buck teeth, and a voice like a foghorn. And that's just how he saw himself. More than once, some girl he didn't even know would walk up to him and say, "You're Larry Valentine's brother? But he's so cute!"

Some guys who lacked the kind of looks that girls admired — most girls anyway — were able to make it up on the sports field. Henry was not one of those. He was slow and uncoordinated, nothing at all like his older brothers including the eldest, 20-year-old Bradley, who had just gotten married. Henry lacked in looks and athletic ability, so he tried music. He had been playing guitar since he was eleven and took up bassoon beginning in the seventh grade.

Many of his classmates thought Henry was a natural-born bassoon-player. They might say that a comical guy like Henry should be playing a comical instrument, and, to them, nothing looked or sounded as ridiculous as a bassoon. To some extent, Henry identified with the bassoon. Mr. Spencer, the music director at Brookhurst, was very pleased that someone — *anyone* — would be willing to play the eccentric woodwind, so Henry was welcomed into the beginning band that fall and, by the second semester, he had advanced to the intermediate band.

For as long as he could remember, Henry loved humor. His dad had been bringing *MAD* magazines into the home since Henry was three years old and by the time he could read when he was six, he would pore over every issue of the periodical that he could get his hands on. He loved jokes and quips and seldom wasted an opportunity to say something smart and snappy or what he thought was smart and snappy. He also learned to appreciate when the joke was on him. His greatest pleasure was getting laughs. When his third-grade teacher wrote "Henry has a delightful sense of humor. You're fortunate!" on his report card, it was worth more to him than any A's or B's.

A few weeks into seventh grade, the school announced that any students wishing to organize clubs were encouraged to do so. There had been a French Club, a Latin Club, a Stamp and Coin Club, and, of course, a Chess Club at Brookhurst since the day the school opened. One girl in his reading class raised her hand and suggested that a vocabulary club would be a good idea. Although Henry prized his extensive (for a twelve-year-old) vocabulary, he did not think that such a club would be any fun. His idea of fun was humor. Instead of suggesting a Humor Club in class, he ran the idea past a few of his friends: Artie, Hans, Adam, and Ernie.

"What kind of club is it? Do we just tell jokes or something?" asked Tony.

"I guess. I don't know for sure, but I like the idea. I like humor."

Later that evening, Henry told his mom about his idea.

"What kind of club is it?"

"It's a humor club, you know."

"No, I don't know. Just boys sitting around and telling jokes or something?"

"I'm not sure yet. But I want to be in a club, and I want it to be my club."

The Humor Club was established and, as soon as it had seven members and a faculty advisor (reading teacher, Mr. Cordson), its charter was approved by the school. It met once a month. One of the boys suggested that they justify their existence by publishing a joke book, but nothing ever came of it. Mostly, they just sat around and told jokes for a half hour and then adjourned. No more justification was needed. Early in the second semester, they had their last meeting, and by luck, the yearbook photographer was there to capture their picture for the annual, which was given out in June. That was some accomplishment in Henry's eyes. It was the best joke of all.

But joke or not, Henry's club didn't make the right kind of impression on the girls. Not a single girl was interested in joining his club. That was just as well, as some of the jokes Adam was fond of telling came out of his dad's girlie magazines. But still, girls laughed just as often as boys, if not about the same things. Henry struggled to understand that nature of humor and what it was that made people laugh.

In the eighth grade, Henry had tried out for junior varsity basketball, but was cut from the team ten minutes into the first try-out. When track season started, he figured he could find a spot on the roster running the three-quarter mile. The race was as much for endurance as speed and since

Henry's naturally slow running could not make winning a sprint remotely possible, he could manage three laps around the track if he could keep an even pace and just turn it on during the last two-hundred-twenty yards. Just getting to the second lap before the front runner started the third was an achievement for any slow kid.

So, in January, Henry made the team. The thirteen-twenty did not attract many eighth graders. There were eight track meets against other junior high schools in the Anaheim Union High School District during the season and Henry ran in all of them. To say he ran is not to say that he ran well. Inevitably, in every race, he finished last or next-to-last, with the sole exception of his one inexplicable triumph at Trident Junior High near the end of the track season.

The eighth-grade thirteen-twenty unit consisted of Bobby Ramirez, Artie Woods, and Henry. Bobby was a great runner who ran barefoot and had a cool gimmick of pulling off his jersey on the last lap when he would invariably finish first. Henry's friend Artie came in third at most of the meets.

One day, Artie asked Henry a simple question. "Why do you run at all if you're always going to finish last?"

"I do my best."

"Do you? I'm not so sure. You ever notice Bobby looks like he's ready to barf when he's done? You look like you could go another three laps. You're hardly sweating at all?

"When we're at Trident on Thursday, try to keep pace with me. If you feel like passing me, go ahead. Just don't get too far ahead. If you get winded or something, slow down a little. But try to stay ahead of whoever is behind you. Just try it. I want to see you do it."

So, Henry tried it. From the starting gun, he kept himself in the middle of the hunt, staying right behind Artie who was trailing a kid from Trident. He must have provoked Artie because by the beginning of the last lap, his friend had pulled ahead of the Trident boy into second place and then Henry stayed right behind Artie and was in third while Trident's front-runner fell back into fourth. It may have been that the Trident runners weren't very good, but Henry was driving himself as he had never done before and his teammates on the sidelines were yelling, "Go, Henry!" The kid was ready to collapse when he crossed the finish line a few paces behind Artie who finished second, the first time ever. Bobby, of course, had already broken the tape and was hunched over with his hands on his knees, getting his breath back.

The Trident team was scratching their collective heads in wonderment over what happened next. This goofy kid who finished third was mobbed by his teammates and carried on the shoulders of the guy who always came first in the shot put. Then they paraded around the field as if they had just won the Olympics or something. Henry was barely conscious of the celebration since he had not even begun to get his breath back. Even his brother Larry, who had finished first on more than one occasion for the ninth grade thirteen-twenty squad, never was accorded such a triumph. But Larry was as enthusiastic as all the others in honoring his brother. If that was a golden moment, it did not prevent Henry from finishing next to last the following week when he ran in the final track meet of the season.

Henry had worked his way up to advanced band in the eighth grade, playing bassoon. He was a much better musician than an athlete but the girls in school did not see orchestra members in the same light as they did the boys on the sports teams. And as much as Henry liked music, and playing the bassoon, he liked girls even more.

Music festival season was over, and Henry had earned a bronze medal when he decided to drop out of the band at the last quarter term. The music teacher, Mr. Spencer, was notably disappointed by Henry's decision because bassoon players were hard to come by. Mr. Spencer tried a couple of arguments to get Henry to remain an active musician but was unable to persuade the kid to change his mind. "Well, we'll sure miss you, Mike." Mr. Spencer could never get Henry's name right.

Henry had no confidence in his baseball skills — with good reason — even though he was a huge baseball fan. So, he decided to try tennis. There was a spot for him on the eighth-grade tennis team, even though he had never played the game before, had no natural ability, and was not particularly interested in the sport. All the same, anything was better than the drudgery of everyday physical education class.

The tennis courts at Brookhurst were right next to the junior varsity baseball diamond, and several times during a match, the tennis teams would have to duck because a foul pop-up was coming their way. Almost as often, the baseball team would have to call time out when one of Henry's errant volleys would end up on the ball field. If Henry ever won a single game against a rival player, it was considered a miracle, as most of his matches ended up six to zero in the other guy's favor. Anybody might think that Henry had learned from his athletic ineptitude, but he had plans for playing football in the fall.

Then, one day, in the middle of the tennis season, the school administration announced that any student considering running for school office for the 1967-68 school year could pick up a petition in the office. One might think that Henry would not be looking for another way to humiliate himself, but it never paid to underestimate the kid's determination.

Henry had assisted his brother Larry in a successful campaign for Student Body President the year before, so he figured his electioneering experience was an advantage that he might have over any other candidate. Why not run for the same office? Henry rethought the possibility when he heard his friend Jim Warren was already getting his petition for the top spot. Then he learned that another guy, Wesley Walcott, was also trying for Student Body President. Although neither candidate was a star athlete, they dressed cooler, were better-looking, and, in every way, more conventional than Henry, as far as he could tell about such things. He didn't relish the competition.

The office of Ninth Grade Class President did not carry the prestige of school president, but neither did it carry the responsibility. (It should be pointed out here that at the time, the Anaheim district had three-year high schools and three-year junior highs.) Besides, Henry would not have to canvass votes from seventh graders when it was hard enough to get kids from his own grade to sign his petition. The rules required that every candidate for class office must obtain a minimum of forty signatures. When Henry picked up his petition, the principal's secretary informed him that he was the first student to announce his candidacy.

The fact that Henry was, so far, the only student in the race did not make it any easier to get kids to sign his petition. "Who else is running?" was the inevitable question. "Nobody yet," was the only answer he could give. So, except for his friends, nobody else was ready to commit his signature to the petition. By the second day, Henry's status as sole candidate changed when Sylvia Shepard filed.

Sylvia had sat next to Henry in seventh grade English class and was always nice to him, and even laughed at his quips. She was a bubbly blonde with big hazel eyes and was better developed than most of the other girls in his class. Henry was prone to falling in love but, for some reason, Henry did not fall in love with Sylvia as he might have done in another instance. Perhaps it was her too-full lips or too-short nose. Whatever it was, when Henry exchanged pleasantries with the young lady, the enjoyment was all from the neck up. It was unlikely that Sylvia felt any attraction to Henry either.

It had never occurred to Henry that his opponent would be a girl, especially a girl that he liked. When somebody asked him what he thought of the other candidate, Henry had to answer truthfully. "I like Sylvia. She's a nice girl. She might make a good president." In her turn, Sylvia said pretty much the same thing about Henry. It may have been the most uncontentious election ever.

In fact, when the designated period of signature-gathering was over, and Henry had accumulated fifty signatures, Sylvia and he sat together and compared petitions. Sylvia had more names than Henry, so she generously crossed out any signatures on her petition that were also on Henry's, thus assuring that there would be two candidates for Ninth grade president on the ballot.

For the top two spots, Wesley Walcott and Roger Willits would be running unopposed. Jim Warren and his friend Stan Helms, who was petitioning for Student Body Vice-President, were both disqualified as the administration were reviewing qualifications. It seemed that all candidates must have at least a 2.5 grade average and have perfect deportment scores to be eligible, and Jim and Stan were deficient in one or the other. So, Wesley and Roger were shoe-ins.

Henry was his own campaign manager and began to make posters out of some old *Life* magazines and "Peanuts" Sunday comic strips he had accumulated. Pasting pictures of movie and TV icons along with Snoopy and Charlie Brown claiming they were voting for Henry appeared on walls and posts throughout the school. Some kids said that it was wrong to use those images without permission; that it was a big lie, in fact. But Henry persisted and the posters stayed up, along with a few that had psychedelic lettering that Henry had copied from music magazines. Henry was hoping that he might gain a few votes just by name recognition associated with the posters. Not every kid knew him.

One day, a week before the election, the candidates for all offices were to appear in a school assembly and give a speech on why they should be elected. Henry had no idea why *he* should get their votes; there were no issues, nobody knew exactly what it was the Ninth Grade President did, and nobody really cared. Henry asked President Larry what he should say.

"It's a beauty contest, Henry, but sometimes the ugly girl gets the ribbon."

So, Henry followed his brother's advice. "Thank you. I'm not going to make a long speech. As Ninth Grade president, I will work hard to get more privileges for ninth graders. I will be honored to serve my class." Then he sat down. Several students were heard to say, "That's it? That's his speech? Three crummy sentences?" But Henry was satisfied because some of the other candidates told jokes that received either groans or nothing, and one girl, Connie Grunenfeld, who was running for school treasurer, said that she would cry if she didn't get elected.

After the assembly, when Henry was leaving the gymnasium with the crowd, a little seventh grade girl walked up to him and sneered, "Eeew! I'm not voting for you!" Henry ignored her, knowing that his name would not even be on the ballot they gave her since she was not in his class. But he wondered if any eighth graders would not vote for him only because he was tall, pimply, had a funny voice, and wore eyeglasses.

That quarter, Henry had taken journalism as an English elective and was allowed to write for the school newspaper, *The Spartan Shield*. Mr. Older, the teacher, was satisfied with Henry's writing ability right away. He praised Henry's first article about an eighth grader tossing a no-hit shutout for the Spartan junior varsity baseball team. Henry wanted to write about the election, but Mr. Older reminded him that the news is impartial. Larry's friend Dale Minestrone was staff cameraman and was assigned the task of photographing the candidates in the quad, one each of Wolcott and Willits, since they were running unopposed, and a side-by-side of Henry and Sylvia.

Two days before the election, the *Shield* ran the pictures on the front page and Henry had a feeling that the race was probably over. His bucktoothed grin, the sunlight shining off his spectacles, his hair looking uncombed; all this Henry knew did not make him look good. That was nothing compared to how Sylvia looked. He didn't notice it when their picture was being taken, but everybody noticed it when the photo ran: Sylvia wearing a tight sweater and a radiant smile. It was the way the sweater looked that made sure that half the votes, those of the boys, were in the bag for Sylvia.

As the day of the election arrived, Henry was regretting that he had not tried for the top post; it was almost his by legacy, he thought, since brothers Jack and Larry had already been there. And he figured that he would have had a better chance against Walcott who didn't cut such a figure in knits. After the school vice-principal, Mr. Kelsey, announced the winners, and Sylvia was, of course, one of them, Henry asked Mr. Kelsey if he could tell him the vote count.

"Sorry, Henry. We keep that confidential."

Henry's fans and friends commiserated with him, but he was far from inconsolable. He was learning that sometimes the best jokes were on him. He was almost glad that he had lost. His friend Dave walked home with him that afternoon and suggested that there would be other elections. "No, I don't think so. I should concentrate on my strengths. Politics isn't my thing." Dave generously bought him a Coke at the liquor store on La Palma Avenue anyway.

When Henry got home, Larry was sitting in their room, going over his homework assignments. "Hey, Henry. How badly did you lose?"

Henry picked up a copy of the *Shield* off their desk and turned it over to the front page. The boys' eyes focused on the image of the cute girl named Sylvia who was wearing a tight sweater. Henry said, "Sure, Larry. It's right here in black and white. It says I lost by *two points*." Larry's laughter at a joke Henry made at his own expense was the best consolation this defeated candidate could hope for.

Culpepper's Capers
by Bruce Wilson

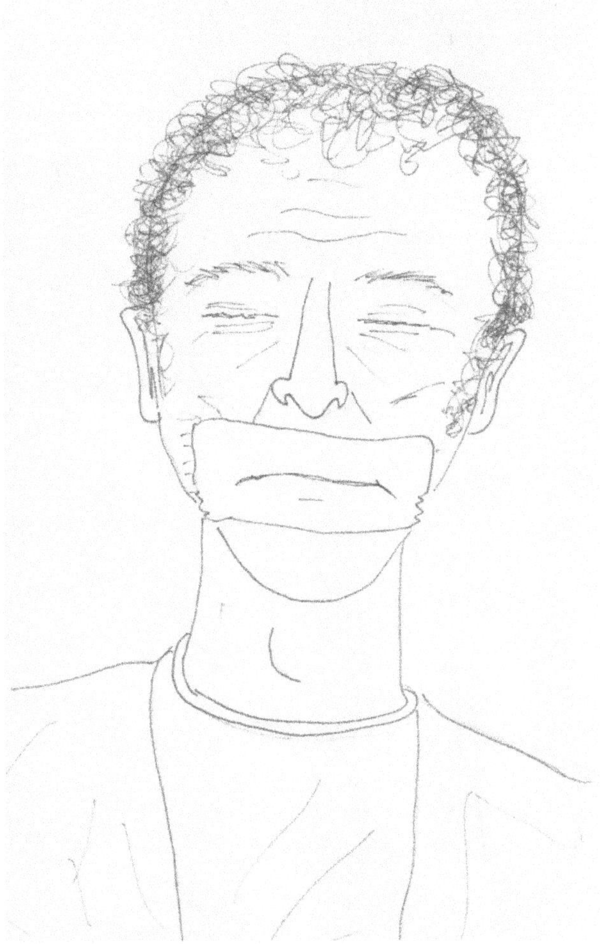

"Pick up the phone, will ya, Harry?"
Harry Prendergast, the proprietor of the Big Bend Bar and Bail Bonds (which specialized in Bourbon and Burgers) leaned over and glanced through the window of his office door. He saw his bartender and part-time secretary, Arlene, standing at the pay phone down the hall. He raised his hand to acknowledge her request, but she didn't notice that only his middle finger showed. Harry was like that.

Arlene left the telephone handset hanging by the cord and walked back behind the bar, yelling once again for Harry to pick up the phone. She asked the two young oil workers if they wanted another beer, this time she used her smoky-smooth tone reserved for flirting, and they each nodded. Harry didn't like it when she flirted. He worried sometimes that a jealous wife would suddenly arrive and cause trouble. But Arlene was usually cautious, at least this time she was. She poured two fresh draughts and ignored Harry as he passed by on his way to the pay phone.

"Thanks, darlin'," Harry said to the back of her bleached-blond head, "and while you're not busy, how about emptyin' the damn ash trays." He continued past the taps and picked up the phone.

"This is Harry," he mumbled.

"Harry, this is Laura Sue from Judge Jessup's office." The voice was formal, stilted, so unlike the woman Harry had dated in high school three decades earlier.

"The judge is right next to your desk, ain't he?"

"Yes, sir, that is correct." She paused and continued. "The judge asked me to advise you that Jim Bob Culpepper has skipped from town in advance of his trial on Monday."

"What?"

With the Judge looking over her shoulder, Laura Sue said, "According to Judge Jessup's notes, one of Sheriff Cree's deputies went by the Rock City RV Resort yesterday and learned that Jim Bob had checked out. The deputy then went to Wanda's house and she didn't know where her son was. Then she laughed and said good luck deputy."

Harry whispered, "crap."

A slight smile crept onto Laura Sue's face. "Roscoe called the DA who told the judge."

Harry slumped against the wall. This was not the Thursday he'd hoped for.

"Harry, are you still there?"

"Yeah, Laura, sorry. Tell the judge I'll be in touch. I gotta find Jim Bob, or Roscoe's gonna have to evict Wanda." He paused and added, "I think my task will be easier than Roscoe's, 'cause Wanda's gonna be madder than hell when she finds out what he did. I gotta go."

After Laura Sue said goodbye, he hung up the phone and headed back past the bar.

"Arlene, finish up there, pour me a shot of Blanton's, and come into the office. We need to talk." He waited until she stood in front of his desk and said, "I gotta go see Wanda Culpepper. Jim Bob's skipped out on his bail." Harry swallowed the rich bourbon in one gulp and let the air slowly drift from his mouth.

"Geez, Harry."

"So, you keep an eye on the bar. I'll be back in a bit, but first I gotta call Roscoe."

Harry dialed the sheriff's direct line and Roscoe answered.

"Roscoe, this is Harry." He paused. "Yes, that Harry, you know I'm the only one in town." After listening to the lawman's wheezy laugh, Harry said, "You heard about Jim Bob, right?"

"Yeah, I did."

"Well, here's the interesting part. He used Wanda's house as collateral on his bond. If he disappears, that means you'll have to evict Wanda."

"The hell you say…"

"Keep your britches on, Roscoe. Give me a day or so to sort this out and to warn Wanda, unless you want to go see her?"

"No thanks, Harry" Roscoe growled.

"Okay, then. I'll let you know what I find."

Harry drove to Wanda's house and knocked on the door.

"Mornin', Harry. What's up?"

"Have you seen your boy? He's skipped town according to the sheriff."

"I thought that's what was going on. One of Roscoe's deputies was here earlier and I told him I haven't seen him since yesterday."

"Well, Wanda, you might wanna think a little harder, 'cause that son of yours used your house for collateral on the bond?"

"Are you fu…" She stopped to take a deep breath. "Are you kidding me, Harry? 'Cause if you are I'll slap you upside the head."

"Nope, Wanda, I'm not. But as soon as I get back to the bar and arrange for Arlene to cover for me, I'll be out looking for him."

"You go ahead and look, but I'll find that sorry kid and make him even sorrier. He'll be in my kitchen tonight or he'll be in the hospital when I get through with him."

"Ooookay, Wanda."

Harry got back in his car, but before he turned the key he glanced back at Wanda standing in the doorway. She looked pissed. *The wrath of Satan was about to come down on Jim Bob*, he thought.

Back at the bar, Harry churned through his options as he entered the small cluttered space known as his office—one desk, two jobs. Most of the time the bar ran itself. Arlene kept him apprised of the inventories such as beer, snacks, produce and bourbon; especially the bourbon. He was famous for having the best in the county.

The bail bond business was more sporadic. Rock City was the county seat, but still small enough that the crime rate was low. The sheriff kept things under control and most incidents never even reached Jessup's courtroom. Bonds seldom exceeded ten thousand dollars, and Harry's savings and the good collateral he required on each case pretty much protected him. But the case against Jim Bob Culpepper was already proving to be the exception.

Culpepper had been raised by his mom after his dad took off with the cashier at his appliance store for parts unknown. The two fugitives had never been heard from again, so Wanda sold the appliance business to one of the greeters at Walmart. She used the proceeds to buy a five-room house not far out of town.

Jim Bob once had a girlfriend, Naomi, but she broke up with him after he got arrested when the sheriff found him with his arm stuck in the bank's night deposit box. Jim Bob wore a plaster cast for six weeks after the incident. Harry almost felt sorry for the kid, but business was business and the law was the law, and he had a job to do.

Jim Bob's latest caper, though, was one good enough to show up in the state capital newspaper (albeit a reprint from the *Rock City Journal*.) The DA, Peter Ashton, *alleged* (although the evidence is specific and overwhelming) that Jim Bob Culpepper did, on the 9th of August, attempt to remove an ATM from the Rock City Bank and Trust property by hooking a logging chain around the ATM and attaching it to the rear bumper of his 1972 Chevrolet pickup. The article went on to say that the attempt was unsuccessful. All the sheriff had to do was follow a deep groove in the street's asphalt pavement after being advised by patrons of the Dairy Queen that they'd seen Jim Bob racing down the street dragging the heavy armored box which screeched along the street. According to one of the DQ customers, "There was a hell of a spark show going on." The article stated that the ATM and logging chain were discovered wrapped around the lighted sign in front of the Holy Redeemer Church, and when the sheriff arrived at Culpepper's residence he found the pickup—minus the bumper. When Jim Bob was confronted with the evidence, he claimed that it was just a prank gone bad. The sheriff was quoted as saying, "Jim Bob, that prank is putting you in the tank."

The ironic thing about Jim Bob's effort, as Roscoe told Harry, was that since it was the end of the month and the oil companies had paid their workers, there wasn't more than sixty dollars left in the machine. "Even if the knuckle head had succeeded, he wouldn't have made enough money to fill up his gas tank," the sheriff said. He went on to tell Harry that the bank's security camera also got a clear, full-face shot of Jim Bob as he looped the chain around the box, hooked it to his rear bumper with a heavy combination lock and drove away.

Most of the folks in town had told and re-told the story in the diner, at the 7-11, in the barber shop and at Hazel's Hair Haven such that it became legendary. Everyone, it seemed, had one more tidbit to add to the story. But today, after Laura Sue's call, Harry wasn't laughing.

Harry sat back in his chair and signaled Arlene to come into the office.

"Have a seat, darlin'."

She pulled the rickety cane back chair away from the desk and heaved a loud sigh, wishing she was at the bar with the oil workers.

"What is it, Harry?"

For a moment, Harry stared at his bartender. He didn't blink or even move his head. Arlene fidgeted, looked away from Harry then pulled a squashed pack of Luckies out of the back pocket of her cut-offs. She lit one of the crumpled cigarettes, inhaled deeply, and blew a cloud of smoke across the desk.

"What?" she said again.

"Wanda didn't know about her house being used as collateral," Harry said.

"Jim Bob just skipped out on his own mom? Hell," Arlene said, "Where would he go? He can't even find the fly on his jeans for cryin' out loud."

"All of that is true, and that's why I need to start looking for him. I need you to run the bar for the rest of the day." Arlene began to shake her head from side to side. "Wait a minute, hear me out. Since this could cost me a lot of money, I'm willin' to pay you overtime, double pay for the rest of the day. It's Thursday, so we won't be real busy. But, I need to be out looking for Jim Bob and you're the only one I trust to watch the bar."

"Geez, Harry, I had plans for tonight."

"With those brain-dead airheads at the bar?"

"Well…"

He watched her consider the offer. "Look Arlene, sometimes we push each other's buttons, don't we?" Arlene nodded. "But I pay you well and have always let you have time off when you needed it." She nodded again. Harry continued. "So, I need your help and I'll make it worth your time. I just can't let that small-town crook disappear and leave his mom homeless."

They talked about the situation for a while longer, then Arlene stood, shook Harry's hand and said he could count on her. He watched her tight cut-offs exit the office and took a very deep breath. Arlene was something else, and he knew it.

The "Happy Daze" trailer park was just a mile or so south of the bar. In Rock City, the trailer park met all of the qualifications for a slum. Most of the mobile homes were not mobile. Their tires had long ago rotted away from the extreme sunshine. The yards grew only clumps of crabgrass which did little to keep the dust down. A variety of fences surrounded each lot—

rusty chain link, broken-down pickets, and the occasional cinder block stack joined by scrap lumber.

Fortunately, Naomi was home and sitting on the narrow steps of the small aluminum trailer, smoking what could have been a joint. Harry parked his car just short of the wire fence and stepped out onto her dried up, dead lawn.

"Harry," she said through her smoke-squinted eyes.

"Hey, Naomi. I need some help."

"Help? What kinda help? I already got a job, Harry." She couldn't seem to focus her eyes on him.

"Yeah, I know. I just need some information. I need to find Jim Bob, Naomi."

"Jim Bob?" she snickered slowly, "I ain't seen that S.O.B. in weeks."

Harry gave her a few seconds before speaking again.

"I figured that, but I thought that maybe you might know some of the places he hangs out." Watching her face consider the situation, he waited. This was becoming more of a challenge than Harry had anticipated.

"What's he done now? Couldn't be much worse than trying to steal an ATM," she said as she looked at her joint and then gazed off into the distance.

"It *is* worse than that. He's run off, skipped out."

"Well, if he's left town, we should declare a holiday," she said as she took a hit off the tightly rolled roach clenched in her fingers.

"I'm with you on that, girl, but he also put up his mom's house as collateral on the bond and if he skips, she'll be homeless."

"Well, that sure sounds like Jim Bob."

"Yep, exactly my sentiments. So, any ideas?"

"Have you been by the recy plant? That's where he was working before the bank job." She couldn't keep the smile from spreading across her face.

"You mean the recycle plant? That's gonna be my next stop."

"He never told me where else he went. I hope for Wanda's sake you find him first." Naomi leaned back against the steps, letting the smoke curl from her lips as she watched Harry cross the yard to his car.

As he pulled away from the trailer, Harry thought, *those two belong together*.

When he arrived at the chain link enclave of the recycling plant, Harry parked next to the corrugated metal Quonset hut that served as an office for the manager, Jerry.

"What's up, Harry?"

"Looking for Jim Bob. Have you seen him today?"

"I haven't seen him since I fired him after his second bank job." Jerry smiled and even chuckled a bit just like Naomi had done. "It's a wonder he lasted as long as he did. The fool couldn't seem to tell the difference between glass and plastic. What an idiot."

"Thanks, Jerry. Give me a call if you see him."

Harry drove around most of Rock City for the next hour or so, up and down all of the streets and through the parking lot of the strip mall looking for Jim Bob's bumper-less truck. He went by the DQ, the 7-11, and even stopped by the Sheriff's Office to see if Jim Bob had decided to turn himself in. He hadn't.

Shortly after eight, his cell phone—a flip phone with a broken hinge—buzzed in his pocket.

"Harry? Arlene. Wanda just called and said she needs to see you at the house right away."

"Okay, thanks. Is everything okay at the bar?"

"I'm fine. Just get over to Wanda's. She's hot about *something*."

It took Harry about ten minutes to drive across town and when he pulled up into the driveway, Wanda stepped out onto the porch. She waved Harry in and went back into the house, letting the screen door slam behind her.

"Crap," Harry mumbled, "What now?"

He walked through the small hallway and into Wanda's clean kitchen. What he saw next surprised the hell out of him. Jim Bob Culpepper was sitting on one of his mother's red vinyl and chrome dinette chairs. An entire roll of silver duct tape had been used to keep him immobile. Each of his ankles was triple wrapped to the chair legs. Even his wrists were bound to the seat bottom with the sticky, silver tape. A band of tape fully three layers thick went across his mouth, nose and cheeks, then wrapped around the back of his neck. Then, as it arrived again at the front of his head it crisscrossed his forehead. The only parts of Jim Bob's face Harry could see were his bulging eyes, two tiny airholes, and a triangular patch of very purple skin at his widow's peak.

"Good god, Wanda. What have you done?" He took a step back.

"Here's your boy, all taped up nice and neat."

"Crap, Wanda. What do you want me to do with him?"

"Before you say any more, Harry, I'd like you to pull the tape off this sorry excuse for a son. And don't you dare be gentle. If he loses some of that long hair or skin off his lips it won't be anything as bad as what's gonna happen to him in *prison*!"

Wanda leaned over and, nose to nose, she looked into her son's eyes. "You hocked my house, *my* house, so you wouldn't have to spend a week in jail and then…" She stopped. "Do it now, Harry. Rip the tape off his face and I'll let *him* tell you where he's been and what he was doing."

He reached toward Jim Bob and the boy flinched. Harry's inclination *was* to be gentle, but Jim Bob's skipping out on Wanda and nearly putting Harry deep in debt quickly got rid of that notion. Jim Bob squirmed and groaned as Harry picked at the edge of the tape. When Harry got a flap loose, he put his other hand on top of Jim Bob's head and tugged on the free end. The first two layers of tape came apart easily, although much of the boy's long hair down his neck—he wore a mullet—came off in chunks. When Harry got to the last layer, the one attached to Jim Bob's lips, he pulled quickly, wanting to be done with the torturous task.

What happened next would have made a great scene in a 1970s horror flick. The action, the sound effects, and the screaming dialogue coupled with the visuals might even have earned an Oscar.

Jim Bob was a fright. He had two-inch wide bloody stripes across his forehead and cheeks. His lips bled profusely, having lost their top layer of skin. His hair had come off in huge chunks—right down to the scalp in some places—and his eyebrows existed only at the bridge of his nose.

But it was the growling, howling, animal-like roars and cries coming from his chopped-liver mouth that would have sent teenage girls screaming toward the theater lobby. These same shrieks, bellows and unintelligible sounds drove Harry backward and he crashed into Wanda's refrigerator, nearly toppling it. Wanda the tape-winder, moved around her son, yelling and laughing like one of the patients up at the sanitarium. Still firmly taped to the chair, Jim Bob hopped across the linoleum. Even Wanda's quick steps didn't prevent her from getting bumped and jostled by him as he bounced around the small room.

The scene ended with a bang when Jim Bob collided with Harry as the bar owner bounced off the refrigerator and rebounded into it again. Jim Bob's ride ended as the chair leaned precariously backward and then tipped over forward and his face bounced twice off the floor.

Harry finally moved away from the refrigerator and looked at Wanda. She glanced up from rubbing her bruised knees and then they both looked down at the silver-taped lump that was Jim Bob Culpepper.

Looking at Wanda once more, Harry leaned over Jim Bob and pulled the chair up. He could see the young man's chest moving, his eyes gazing off in different directions, and his shredded lips trying to form words.

"Crap," Harry said. "He is going to look like hell come Monday. The judge is gonna…"

"Oh, shut up, Harry." Wanda moved directly in front of Jim Bob and stared into his flickering eyes and laughed. "You want me to tell you where he's been?"

"Not right now, Wanda," Harry mumbled.

Wanda ignored Harry and told him how Jim Bob had decided to spend all of his money on this girl (she'd said 'whore') across the county line. "He figured it'd be a long time 'til he had a chance to get with a female, so he showed up at the rusty old trailers over there, went inside and …" Wanda started giggling, then struggling to catch her breath. Sucking in huge gulps of air, she continued after a hiccup or two. "He went inside, asked for this girl and the old woman who runs the place said…" Wanda roared, tears rolled down her face and she looked at Jim Bob then at Harry and said, "She said, 'We're closed.'"

"Huh?" said Harry.

"She said, 'we're closed.' My bonehead boy couldn't even pull off one final caper right."

"Huh?" Harry repeated.

"They were closed, damn it!"

Harry walked out onto the porch, opened his cell and called Roscoe. When he answered, Harry said, "Don't ask any questions, Roscoe. Just get on out here to Wanda's and pick the boy up."

On Monday morning, the energy in Rock City was electric. People scurried along the sidewalks toward the courthouse. Most of them dressed in their Sunday best—it wouldn't do to show up for the trial of the century wearing everyday clothes, no sir. A few enterprising folks had set up tents and were selling everything from bottled water to bags of the county's famous roasted pecans. Even an hour before the proceedings were to begin, there was a line that went all the way down the steps and halfway up the block to the Piggly Wiggly.

Inside the Depression-era courthouse, Roscoe had stationed deputies in strategic spots to control the crowd. Even if folding chairs were set up in the courtroom, the most that could be seated was just short of a hundred; nowhere near enough room for all of the adults trying to get in. The tall double door at the entry was still open, but the deputies managed to keep the late arrivals outside in the hall.

Those lucky enough to be seated inside the courtroom found themselves squeezed tightly together on the oak benches behind the rail separating them from the prosecution and defense tables, the jury box, and the elevated bench where Judge Jessup would preside. His clerk, Laura Sue, was also the bailiff. She sat at a desk just past the defense table making a few notes. She looked up and saw that Harry was in the first row, not ten feet from her. She looked at the barkeeper bail bondsman and winked at him.

Familiar with the courtroom procedures, Harry had arrived early and taken a seat he knew would be close to Laura Sue. He caught her wink and returned one of his own. What pleased him nearly as much was that he was close enough to smell her perfume—the same brand she'd worn in high school. A memory of the two of them in the back seat of Harry's car down by the river flashed across his mind and he shifted in his seat to bring himself into the present.

The defense table was still empty, but across the aisle, the D.A., George Atherton, pulled several stacks of paper from his polished leather briefcase and studied them. Harry looked around at the crowd in the gallery and spotted Jerry from the recycle center. Jerry waved to him, a broad smile on his lips. In the row behind Jerry, sat Helen Pruitt, the proprietor of Helen's Hair Haven. Her highly teased and heavily sprayed hairdo reminded Harry of the helmet he wore when he played football for the Rock City High School Rockets. He saw that Wanda was sitting right behind the table where Jim Bob would face the music and that Naomi was in the back row of benches, leaning much the same way as she'd done against the steps of her trailer, a grin on her lips and her eyes trying to stay focused.

Out in the hallway, what sounded like a murmur of thunder drifted into the courtroom. Then, marching down the center aisle came Jim Bob Culpepper's court-appointed public defender, Vernon "Little-V" Walker. The counselor looked to be about seventeen years old and was wearing a suit that he probably bought at Goodwill. His slight frame and spiky red hair did little to enhance his self-image as a young Perry Mason. Having just graduated from the Amazon Prime Online Law School, this was his first case. But, unfortunately for Little-V, it wasn't his client's first visit to the courtroom.

Shuffling down the aisle behind Walker, Jim Bob Culpepper appeared to not have healed much in the few days since the events at Wanda's. The raw tape wounds on his wrists and ankles were covered by his clothes. Despite the heroic efforts of Helen at her beauty shop, his head was a patchwork of raw wounds and closely clipped hair. The mullet had been replaced by a skin/hair patchwork quilt. What stood out to the gasping crowd—most of whom had only heard the scattered snippets about the fiasco at Wanda's—was the condition of Jim Bob's face. The crisscross tape wounds had taken off the top layer of skin from his cheeks and forehead. His now crusted lips were the color and texture of redwood bark. Jim Bob's eyebrows, what remained of them, looked like dime-size blotches nestled against the bridge of his nose. In essence, Jim Bob Culpepper looked like he'd lost a fight with an angry bobcat. Jim Bob glanced past Wanda sitting right behind him and spotted Helen, who gave him a big thumbs-up and touched her own hair. Jim Bob didn't smile and slowly lowered himself into the chair behind the table.

When the bailiff stood up, the murmuring ceased and the door behind the bench opened.

"All rise!" said Laura Sue, and the portly Judge H.H. Jessup stepped onto the platform and took his seat behind the bench.

With a signal from Jessup, Laura Sue told the courtroom to be seated. Another signal from the judge led her to say, "The First Judicial Court of Rock City is now in session, Judge H.H. Jessup presiding." She went on for a few minutes going through some procedural and house-keeping announcements, then turned to the judge.

"Thank you, Laura Sue." The judge turned to the D.A. and the brand-new lawyer, both of whom had remained standing throughout the bailiff's instructions. "I understand that you, Mr. Walker and the District Attorney, Mr. Atherton, have discussed a possible amendment to the proceedings on today's docket."

"Yes, your honor, we have," squeaked Little-V. Atherton simply nodded.

Jessup asked them to approach the bench where the three men held a whispered conversation. Jim Bob slumped back in his chair and was summarily slapped on the back of his head by Wanda.

"Sit up you bum," she whispered.

"Oww," is what the first three rows of the gallery heard from Jim Bob.

After Jessup and the attorneys had finished their discussion, the judge looked toward Jim Bob and spoke to him, his gravelly voice carried clearly to the sides and back of the gallery. But he held up when Naomi shouted, "Praise the Lord."

"Order in the court," he said, pounding his gavel on the block.

Turning back toward the lawyers, Jessup continued, "Mr. Walker, would you and your client please stand?" They responded immediately, or as quickly as Jim Bob could move his aching muscles. "Jim Bob Culpepper, your attorney has advised me that you wish to change the plea you gave me at the arraignment from "Not Guilty" to "Nolo Contedre. Do you understand what that means?"

Jim Bob nodded and Little-V elbowed him in the side. With an audible groan, Jim Bob said something that sounded like, *"meshburdonner."* Everyone, including Judge Jessup, assumed he meant "yes, your honor."

"Very well, in light of the change in plea, there will be no jury selection in this case." A disappointed murmur spread across the room. It quickly ceased when Jessup's frown became visible. He continued. "Then, Mr. Jim Bob Culpepper, I would like you to walk over to the spot my bailiff will point out to you."

Jim Bob stepped behind Little-V and approached the judge's bench. Laura Sue indicated where he should stand and said that he should remain still and not speak unless asked to do so by the judge. The big, battered boy nodded and looked up at the scowling man in the black robe.

"Jim Bob, this is not the first time you've been in my court, is it?"

Culpepper looked at Laura Sue who nodded at him. He turned back to the judge and said, very slowly and not very clearly, *"Noburdonner."*

"No, it is not. When you were six years old you stood in that very same spot between your mother and your father and confessed to playing with matches that started a grassfire which nearly burned down the Thornton Elementary School." He looked at his notes and continued. "Then, when you were twelve, you were here because a number of your neighbors claimed that you had been throwing rocks at their pets. Do you recall these events?"

Those in attendance heard something close to "yes, your honor."

"Each of these cases ended up costing your parents substantial fines and time away from their workplace." He looked into the audience and spotted the bank manager. "Now, it seems that you have decided to expand your criminal activities to felonies. Earlier this year you were accused of trying to rob the Rock City Bank by reaching into and subsequently getting your arm caught in the night deposit box. If that wasn't enough, not two weeks ago, you decided that you'd abscond with the single ATM in our town by towing it away chained to the back of your pickup truck." He paused again. "It is this most recent action on your part that draws us all here today."

Jessup looked through his notes for a bit and then glanced around the courtroom.

"Mr. Culpepper, I must say that the people of Rock City would, except for the humor you provide, be happy if I sent you to the state penitentiary for a long, long time. Not only did you intend to rob the bank for a second time, you used your mother's home as collateral for the bail bond and decided it was okay to make her homeless"

Jim Bob flinched when he heard Wanda let loose with a fiery stream of cusswords.

"I know," said the judge, "that your present condition was not a result of being mishandled by anyone in the jail and that your poor mother has tried to raise you properly ever since your father…well, ever since your father left town. It is not her fault that you have attempted to be a one-man crime wave."

Tears began to drip from the corners of Jim Bob's bloodshot eyes.

"Mr. Walker, will you please join your client up here?"

When Little-V stood next to Jim Bob, the judge said, "It is the order of this court that James Robert Culpepper will be remanded into the custody of his mother following the completion of today's trial. Jim Bob, you will be required to wear an electronic ankle bracelet for the next two years. I had hoped that we could use the rusty iron shackles from the old days, but the folks at the museum wouldn't take them from the display. You will wear this bracelet 24 hours per day or face a change in sentence to five years in the state penitentiary. One more thing, Jim Bob. Since you have so much time on your hands having already been fired from the recycle center, I have found you a job."

Jim Bob looked up at the judge, his painful brow wrinkling and drawing the nubs of eyebrows close to dead center on his forehead. The townsfolk in the gallery sat up in their seats, leaning forward so as not to miss the pronouncement. Wanda watched the back of her son's head. Harry and Laura Sue seemed distracted and were smiling at one another, unaware of the building excitement.

"Beginning tomorrow, you will work forty hours each week, eight hours per day in the product safety department of…"

A buzz of excitement, almost physical in nature, carrying the same electric energy as this morning, seemed to spread across the room.

"…the brand-new 3M Duct Tape factory on the state highway. This court is adjourned!"

Contiguity
by Chas Wilson

Darryl slid three quarters into the vending machine and weighed his options. His shoulders wearily dropped and he let out an anguished sigh. The surgery was going to take hours, and she would be in recovery and rest for even more hours until he could see her.

He couldn't wrap his mind around the concept of surgery and didn't want to picture Penny being cut open! He needed to distract himself with something while the doctors did what he prayed was the best they could possibly do. He could sit in the waiting room, eat more vending machine crap, and read three-year-old magazines, but he thought that he would drive himself mad with worry doing that.

If he only had something to divert himself from his despairing thoughts, to fill the waiting with something that made him confident, or at least not negative. He could go home, wait there, and come back later – this afternoon, maybe, but probably tomorrow. But what to do at home? There's nobody there and he needed to decompress, maybe verbally work through this.

That's it; he had to talk it out. Now. When he was young and things got "bad" at home, he and his brother, Dana, would take a walk and sort things out. He could go out to the Marine base at Twentynine Palms, spend a few hours with Dana, and be back here at the hospital by this evening, if necessary. Even though it was early morning, he called Dana.

"Captain Cooper."

"Hey, Dana, Darryl. Is it too early to call?"

"Are you kidding me? I've been up for three hours. What's up?"

"They just took Penny into surgery and I probably won't be able to see her until tomorrow. Her parents are here in case any decisions need to be made. I really need to talk, man. Can you break free for a few hours? I can be there by eleven."

"Come on out. We'll take a walk in the park. Call me when you get close."

He said goodbye to Penny's parents and was soon heading east on the 91. It was a typical gray, sticky, gritty Southern Cal morning. Not yet hot. He was lucky that traffic was relatively light. It may not be early for Dana, but it was for him. The buzzing sizzle of the traffic and the rising heat was causing him to nod, so he turned on the radio for distraction. He found a station with an ancient top 40 playlist. Most of these old songs reminded him of some event from his past. The one now playing brought him back to one of his first dates with Penny. It was the first time they had kissed.

She had taken him to a Korean BBQ place in Garden Grove, where you grilled your own meat right on the table. He had not eaten Korean before, so was cautiously trying everything. Penny loved it all, especially cabbage kimchi, which she seemed to relish. The evening was light and fun, and Penny's bouncing copper curls and her dazzling blue-green eyes charmed him as much as her tinkling laughter. He was smitten. At the end of the evening, he had walked her to her front door and leaned in to brush her lips with his when she blew him away with the most unforgettable kiss back. Her tongue was smooth, very wet, spicy, and warm. She pulled away with a quick, "Thanks for a great time, see you soon," and she was into the house. He was paralyzed for a moment and then staggered back to his car. Wow!

He never missed a chance to repeat that experience.

Their romance progressed like all young romances: a little risk, a little turbulence, discovered delights, new feelings, and new smells. Penny often applied a scent to her hair that, at first, made him think of Christmas. It was the warm kitchen smell of oranges and cloves. It was winter crispness and a crackling fire. He had no idea that one could fall in love with scent! When her hair became undone and she shook it out or fluffed the curls, his heart was grabbed and thrust into a vortex of emotion, thumping with ecstasy.

They grew closer in college. She breezed through, with the same ease that she had in high school. Her study habits were anchored in the safe harbor of a dependable and loving home life. Her routine was as constant as the tides. She dispatched her studies quickly, so she could spend more time with Darryl. Darryl's progress was conversely turbulent and choppy. He lived half of the time with his mother and her second husband, the other half with his father and his father's third wife. Dana and he had six step- and half-siblings, all of whom struggled just as they did with the lack of routine in their respective homes.

A few years later, once Darryl and Penny had graduated from college and entered the workforce, Penny began broaching the subject of marriage. Darryl defensively parried:

"Why don't we just move in with each other?"

"You know I can't do that."

"Won't do that."

"I want to have children, Darryl, and can't do that if we're not married."

"We could live with each other and get a couple of dogs instead."

"No, we couldn't"

The truth was, Darryl was afraid of marriage and afraid of having children. Penny saw how good traditional marriage could be and Darryl saw instead how fraught with the pitfalls it could have. They couldn't reconcile their differences, but maintained their love for one another, although they kept separate homes. They saw each other daily, but each one slept alone at night. Penny brought up the subject of marriage occasionally, but Darryl found a way of dodging the question or slipping out of the discussion. Nonetheless, Penny was tenacious, and presented the idea with the most sedulous care. She had a way of lightly stroking his forearm with her fingertips when she spoke with him. That made it even harder for Darryl to sidestep her questions or avoid committing himself. She wanted to have children and she wanted Darryl to be their father and her husband, but how long could she suffer a continued negative response?

On an ordinary day, with nothing to distinguish it from the others, Penny didn't feel up to spending the evening with Darryl. She bowed out with a flat, "I'm not quite myself. I'll just spend a quiet night taking it easy." Nothing more. They later marked this episode as the moment that everything changed. It was an inauspicious beginning; in a matter of days she was diagnosed with a terrible cancer. Soon thereafter she had to suffer in turn through chemotherapy, radiation, and today, surgery. Through it all, she maintained an incredibly positive attitude, especially when Darryl was at her side.

But Darryl wasn't at her side; he was on Highway 62, just outside of Yucca Valley. He had already committed to meeting with Dana and had driven for a couple of hours, yet he was feeling that this may not have been the best idea and felt himself being pulled back to the hospital. He called Dana.

"I'll be there in a few. Where are you?"

"Meet me at the sandwich shop on Adobe Road by Indian Trail. We'll pick up some sandwiches and drinks, then go in my car out to the park."

They linked up and headed into the park. Dana made sure Darryl had a hat. As soon as they got out of the car and started walking, it was obvious why; the late morning sun was merciless. They stopped near Skull Rock and ate their sandwiches. After lunch they continued walking farther into the park. It was blazing hot and getting hotter. Dana was used to it but still carried plenty of water. He handed two bottles to Darryl. They talked a lot about Penny and her illness. Darryl also brought up the question of marriage.

"Look Darryl, I'm probably the last guy in the world to give advice about marriage. Hell, I took the easier route and joined the Corps. Seriously, you know I think Penny is an incredible person and would be an incredible wife. If I was ever going to get married, it would be to someone like Penny. She wouldn't let you screw up the marriage. After she gets through with this cancer shit – and she will – you two will work out what's best.

They walked silently for a while. Darryl stopped to drink some water. It tasted like Penny's kiss! A second swig didn't dissuade him. He offered his bottle to Dana.

"Taste this. What does it taste like?"

Dana took a drink then tilted his chin down slightly, knitted his brow, and looked over the top of his sunglasses. "It tastes like water. You Okay?"

"Yeah, fine."

They ambled along the desert path, each with his own thoughts. The desert air was still; there was no movement, no wind at all. The only action was the vibration of the heat on their skin. But then Darryl felt a bitter cold icy chill that had sprung up from behind and leaped about him. It tickled his arms and neck with a light stroking and started his teeth chattering. Then it stopped. Then it started again, this time with an accompanying familiar fragrance – oranges and cloves. He croaked to Dana,

"Did you feel that?"

"Feel what?"

"That cold breeze."

"I wish."

"How 'bout the smell?"

"What smell?"

"Forget it."

They wandered farther into the desert. The heat was producing waves that shimmered off the ground. The effect was a quivering and shuddering canvas of muted color, except for that swaying and shaking russet-colored bush ahead. As he approached it, Darryl glanced up and saw that it was Penny! But then she vanished and what had been her was a Joshua tree. He stumbled and teetered, drank some more water, and sensed that she had kissed him again.

"So, what are you gonna do, Darryl? Darryl? Darryl, are you okay?"

"Yeah, I'm okay. What did you say?"

"We better head back to the car. It's too hot out here."

"Yeah, it's hot. Hot…"

They turned about and headed back from where they had come, when Darryl's cell phone tone sounded. He looked down and saw that the call was from Penny! *She's out and well enough to call!* He slid it to answer.

"Darryl, come back!"

"I will! I'm heading back now!"

"Darryl, come back and marry me!"

"I will, Penny, I will!"

Darryl had slowed and fallen quite behind Dana. Dana turned and called back,

"What are you doing? Are you okay?"

"I'm talking to Penny. She called me."

"Oh, jeez, Darryl," Dana moaned and ran back to him. "Oh, man!" Dana put his arms around his brother and said, "Darryl, there is no cell phone service out here in the park. It's a dead zone. We gotta get you out of here."

"I mean it, Dana, she called me!"

They walked as quickly as they could. They didn't speak again until they passed Skull Rock. Darryl again insisted that Penny had called him. Dana just said, "Let's keep moving." As soon as they got to the car, Dana's cell phone buzzed. It was from the Regiment.

"Sir, this is Staff Sergeant Rodriguez. There's a guy from Anaheim who has called three times. He wants you to call him. Says it's important."

Dana had Darryl sit in the shade for a while until his car's air conditioner kicked in. The guy calling from Anaheim was Penny's dad. Dana called him.

"Dana, I've been trying to reach Darryl, but can't. That's why I called you. Penny passed away during surgery this morning."

- 116 -

Henry And The Latest Rage
by Howard Wilson

Sixteen-year-old Henry had not given much thought to what he wanted for his birthday when his dad asked him about it a few days before the big day. Not that it was going to be a big day in the Valentine household, as everybody else had already had more than sixteen birthdays, Henry being the youngest of six kids, all but one of which still lived at home. His brother Larry had turned seventeen two months earlier, and Henry had no recollection of there even being a cake for dessert that night. It was probably just the usual "cookies and ice cream" or "ice cream and cookies." And if Larry got a gift from the parents, Henry wasn't sure he could remember what it was.

The more Henry thought about it, the less he could come up with an idea. It wasn't that he had no desire for material objects. He frequently blew more than half of his five-dollar-a-week allowance on 45 rpm records or posters or incense holders or other psychedelic souvenirs that were popular. But those were relatively inexpensive items and Henry's dad was hinting at something that may cost as much as twenty bucks.

The one thing that Henry lacked was clothing. His school wardrobe consisted of pocket tees in a variety of colors, 501 Levi's, and desert boots. For the cold days of November and December, Henry would put on an old jacket his parents gave him for Christmas when he was an eighth grader. It kept him warm enough, but it was not the sort of thing that would be advertised in the underground newspapers — like the *L.A. Free Press* that he had hidden in his sock drawer. Moreover, since summer was only two months away, a jacket was not a necessity, and a good one may have been more than his dad would be willing to pay for.

Then Henry had a revelation. He remembered seeing a pair of knee-high moccasins in his size at the Hardy's shoe store in the Buena Park shopping center. They were buff colored with fringe on top and had long, leather laces. As far as Henry knew, nobody at Savanna High, where he was a sophomore, had worn anything like them to school. They looked like something the kids at the rock music festivals would wear, having seen pictures of them in the news magazines. He remembered that they were only $16.99, a figure his dad would be likely to pay without blinking. So, on Friday, Henry's dad drove him to the mall and Henry was the proud owner of what the shoe clerk called "Apache boots."

When he brought them home and showed them to Larry, he expected an enthusiastic response. But Larry only said, "Those are cool, Henry. Have you tried them on yet?"

"Yeah, I tried them on in the store and they fit fine."

"Have you walked around in them?"

Henry looked at Larry's face, trying to see what his brother was leading up to. "Why do you ask that?"

"I understand that they take some getting used to if you've been wearing regular shoes. Heavy soles and support and stuff you get with your desert boots and tennies. Moccasins are like slippers." Larry had obviously been talking to their older brother Jack who had sold shoes from time to time and was currently employed at the C.H. Baker shoe store for ladies at the Anaheim Plaza.

So, Henry pulled the Apache boots on over his calves, stood up, and paced the floor in the bedroom. Larry was right. They were comfortable enough on the bedroom carpet, but they did feel a little flimsy to feet that were accustomed to arch support. Henry felt his toes curl and his heels shift a little back and forth. "Aren't there inserts or something I could stick in there?"

"I wouldn't," Larry said. "Your toes would get crowded and after a while they'd start to hurt. Just walk around in them till you get used to the feel. That's all you can do. By the way —" Larry turned and handed his younger brother a couple of one-dollar bills. "Happy birthday."

Dinner that evening was more festive than usual with spareribs and baked potatoes and strawberry shortcake for dessert. The whole family was there except brother Brad who was married, on active duty in the Navy reserves, and stationed in the Philippines with Nanette, his wife of two years. There was some gratification in having a gathering and being made much of, even though everybody wandered off right after dinner.

Henry frequently spent his Friday evenings following dinner walking by himself the mile or so to the West Fullerton Center, a large strip mall just north of Anaheim. This time he pondered over whether he might try out his new footwear for the trek, to sort of break them in. His feet felt as awkward as Larry had suggested they would and less than halfway up his street, he decided to turn back and change to his regular shoes. He knew he would have to get used to the different feel of his moccasins, but the idea of walking back from Thrifty drug store with sore feet was not something he was ready to face.

Later that night, and several times that weekend, Henry tried walking in his new Apache boots, sometimes pacing the living room, other times walking back and forth across his backyard patio. By Sunday night he felt conditioned enough to wear his birthday gift to school the next day. The only question was whether his trouser legs should be worn inside or outside. At last, he decided that he should tuck his jeans into his Apache boots, otherwise nobody would see how cool he was.

At this time in his life, Henry was coming to terms with how he looked. He knew his goofy baby face, all buck teeth and black-framed glasses, was not to his advantage as far as romance was concerned. He was also aware that having reached a hair under six feet in height was a good thing. At least, nobody looked down on him. He would have liked his ash-blonde hair to be longer, as the current fashion dictated, but his old man had a prejudice against long hair on boys. One thing he was aware of: there were girls out there, pretty girls, who had ugly boyfriends. It stood to reason that a boy's looks were not as important as how he carried himself, how he presented himself. Confidence. That was the key. It was something he knew he needed to work towards.

As Henry waited for the bus to pick him up Monday morning, two other students from his neighborhood looked at his legs but they didn't say anything. It wasn't as if they were friends of his and since he hardly ever spoke to them, he couldn't expect enthusiastic praise for his stylishness. They were the first kids on the bus as Henry's neighborhood was at the farthest reach of his high school's district. Since he was sitting, as usual, in the back of the bus, nobody was likely to spot his footwear. It was just another Monday morning ride to school.

The first class of the day was plane geometry with Mr. Legnano in a Quonset hut. The baby boom and the mad rush to move to Anaheim in the 1950's and 60's had seen to it that there were not enough classrooms to house all the pupils in the area, even with new high schools being built nearly every other year. Fortunately, the Quonset huts were about as large on the inside as the regular classrooms and no less comfortable. Henry sat near the front next to a junior named Randy who was the class clown. Randy would invariably come to class and crow like a rooster when he entered, seconds ahead of the school bell. This time his routine was cut short when he saw Henry's new moccasins.

"Whoa-whoa-wow! Henry, those are *bitchen*!!! You gotta tell me where you bought 'em. Then I can wear them to the next love-in at Hillcrest Park." Randy wasn't holding back. "I can get my psychedelic shirt and my groovy beaded-leather head band and play my green tambourine!" Only Mr. Legnano's appearance a minute later stopped Randy's verbal ribbing, but the whole next ten minutes, he kept looking back at Henry, smiling crazily, pointing to the moccasins, and flashing peace signs while performing a pantomime of smoking a marijuana cigarette. It was more than Henry could stand and even the teacher, who was trying to get the class to pay attention to some mathematical formula, had had enough.

"Mr. Valentine, there are seats in the back of the classroom. I suggest you take one." Mr. Legnano found a formula that was practical: instead of trying to shut Randy up: put the Apache boots and the boy wearing them where few would see them. So, Henry took a desk in the back, right next to Dennis Hasakawa, a fellow sophomore whom he had known since seventh grade. Dennis sat in the desk on Henry's right. He was studying his notes and paused a moment to look at Henry and nod. On Henry's left sat a girl he had never noticed before. She was tall and slender and gave Henry a nice smile. "I like your moccasins," she said, then faced the front. One thing about her smile; it wasn't at all like Randy's. There was nothing sardonic about it.

For his second period class, Henry dressed out for physical education and when he put his school clothes back on, his jeans were over his Apache boots. The rest of the day, he hobbled around campus, his feet getting a little cramped, but not much was said about his new shoes by other students. There was an approving assessment from a senior girl on the school newspaper where Henry was a sportswriter, but most responses were neutral.

Over the next eight weeks, Henry wore the Apache boots to school about eight times, always keeping the high tops covered by his jeans. By the end of the term, he was quite comfortable in them. He remained in the back row of the Quonset hut, struggling with geometry, and found out that he liked Dennis Hasakawa and they became friends of a sort. He also learned the name of the girl on his left, Joyce Farber. They rarely said more than "Hi" to each other, but he got into the habit of sharing his SweeTarts with her. He might have asked her for a date but he didn't have a car or even his driver's license yet.

Henry found the whole hippie scene attractive. He wanted to go to rock festivals, to hang out with groovy chicks, to wear cool threads. When he heard about Woodstock later that summer, he wished they would have something like that in Orange County. There was the "Newport '68" in Costa Mesa, but this summer they moved it to Northridge in L.A. County. In 1968, they had Country Joe and Canned Heat and Jefferson Airplane, and those groups all went to Woodstock. Henry felt that he was missing out on some of the greatest events of his time. He couldn't walk on the moon like the guys from Apollo 11, but he should be able to sit on the lawn in front of a stage and hear Steppenwolf rock out.

Henry's brother Jack had a friend who lived in a house right near the beach in Newport and sometimes they would go there together. Jack's friend Roger lived there with his girlfriend Sandra. It was a cool place to be in the summer and Roger had a lot of LP's that Henry had never listened to before. Jack was twenty-one and Roger was twenty-two and most of their friends who wandered in and out during the day were around the same age. Some of the women were very sexy, Henry thought. It was way better than hanging around his house in Anaheim. Henry was allowed to wander at will along the concrete walk that ran along the beachfront and on one occasion, he entered a boutique and saw the fringed suede leather jacket he dreamed about. He tried it on; it fit. He looked at the price and shook his head. There was no way he could ever afford it and it was impossible that his parents would ever buy one for him.

At the end of July, Henry spent a weekend with his friend Dave who had, two years earlier, moved to Cowan Heights, east of the City of Orange. The boys talked about the upcoming school year when they would both be juniors. Earlier in the summer, Dave and Henry and some Cowan Heights teenage boys had gone to Huntington Beach where Dave met a girl named Nancy. Dave went to Villa Park High and Nancy was going to be a sophomore at Katella in Anaheim. Unlike Henry, Dave had a driver's license and he managed to drop by her house a few times when his parents let him use their second car.

One evening, during this latest visit, Henry accompanied Dave to Nancy's house. Being a third wheel was particularly uncomfortable, and Henry was aware that Nancy didn't care to have him around either. She and Dave wanted to "make out," as the saying went, so Henry decide to take a walk. There was a synagogue around the corner and an evening service was being held. Henry had never been to a synagogue before. He was handed a yarmulke by an usher when he entered. The service was in English and Hebrew and was interesting at first but seemed to go on forever. After about a half hour, Henry walked back to Nancy's and found Dave ready to head back to Cowan Heights.

"Nothing's ever going to come out of this with Nancy," Dave told Henry later that evening. "I have to get a girlfriend from my own high school." Henry thought about the girls in classes when he was a sophomore and imagined that if he could get two or three of them to go on a date with him, at least one would fulfill his dreams of true romance. That Joyce, from his geometry class, for instance. Then he realized that the reality of not having a driver's license would get in the way of any romantic dreams. He was already sixteen and had his learner's permit. What was taking him so long? He would think about that tomorrow.

Henry had brought a few new record albums with him on his visit to Dave's that he had acquired earlier in the summer. One was *Pickin' Up the Pieces* by a group called Poco. It was fun country-rock music. Henry showed Dave the cover of the LP which was a painting of the group. The lead singer was wearing a real cool fringed suede leather jacket that had American Indian symbols on it.

"I saw a jacket that looked just like that in Bullock's over in Santa Ana," Dave said. "You wanna go with me to see it?"

"Sure. I've never been to Bullock's." Bullock's department store was high class to Henry who usually bought his wardrobe at J.C. Penney's and Sears. And the prices at Bullock's were high class too. Then Dave showed Henry the jacket and they both saw the price tag: $109.00. Henry lost all hope He would have to come up with a better idea.

A couple of weeks before fall classes started, Henry reported to Savanna for orientation day. It was time to schedule his classes, get his locker, and pick up health forms for his mom and dad to sign. Late August in Anaheim is always hot, and this day was no different. Nevertheless, the school dress code was in force so shorts and sandals were still forbidden for boys. One kid was sent home to shave off the beard he had managed to grow during the summer. Moustaches were permissible for the first time this year, but beards were out. A couple of other boys were told to get suitable haircuts before the first day of school.

Henry wore his regulation J.C. Penney's pocket t-shirt and Levi's 501 jeans to the orientation, figuring to make it through the ordeal as quickly as possible. By 10:00 a.m., the heat was beginning to get oppressive and wouldn't abate till long after sundown. From a distance, he saw that the line leading up to the eleventh-grade table was very long. Some students were in the process of making the line even longer. Approaching the end, Henry was pleased to see that he would be waiting in line behind none other than Joyce Farber herself.

"Hi, Joyce. How was your summer?" Up to that point, that was the longest speech Henry had ever made to her. For her part, Joyce had said nothing more than the occasional "Hi," since she told Henry that she liked his moccasins the previous April. This hot August day was different.

"Hi, Henry. I wish it was gonna last another month. I can't believe school is gonna start up again in just two weeks."

The two of them jumped from one subject to another in their thirty minutes of conversation. From music to movies to school subjects, they found that they had several things in common. While they were getting to know each other, Henry was doing a physical appraisal and he liked what he saw. Joyce was tall for a girl and slender in an athletic way. She wore her soft brown hair long and slightly rolled, had hazel eyes, and a long nose that went well with her high cheekbones. Henry decided that she was a pretty girl and was thrilled at the opportunity to know her better. Then he learned that she loved art and was a reader.

"Who's your favorite artist?" Henry asked.

"I like the Pre-Raphaelites, like Rossetti."

"Yeah, they're great. I'm into the Impressionists like Renoir but right now I really like Modigliani."

Then the subject turned to literature. "Have you read *Catcher in the Rye*? No? What about *Catch-22*?"

"You seem to like books with "catch" in the title," Joyce laughed. "I'm reading *Island* by Aldous Huxley right now. It's a wonderful book."

"I read his *Brave New World*. Great novel. Maybe you'll let me borrow *Island* when you're done with it."

"Okay, if you lend me one of your 'catcher' books."

By the end of the morning, Henry and Joyce were friends, as she made sure that they would have biology class together and he arranged for their lockers to be side-by-side. He wanted to buy her a Coke, but the cafeteria was closed. His junior year in high school looked to be promising, even if he never owned a fringed suede leather jacket. His new ambition was to find a cheaper and maybe even better alternative.

That Saturday, Henry's mom drove him to the Buena Park Center and had him pick out some new clothes for the fall. "New" was not really applicable inasmuch as 501 jeans and pocket tees were the norm. Boxer shorts and socks, a belt, and a couple of long-sleeved plaid cotton flannel shirts added to the army-navy store finds he had already bought himself earlier from a nearby surplus store. Last of all was the jacket. With the fringed suede dream necessarily forgotten by this time, Henry decided that a Levi's denim jacket was just the thing. It was within the budget, and it looked cool. Sears had one just his size (36) and if it was a little stiff, it would loosen up eventually from daily wear and weekly washing, he was told. His brother Jack had one and it looked great.

Anaheim Septembers are as hot as in August and the first day of school started moving up from 80 degrees, but Henry wore his Levi's jacket anyway. He was eager to show off his style and was equally eager to see Joyce Farber, hoping to impress her. As he disembarked from the school bus, he noticed that one of the kids getting off in front of him was wearing a fringed suede leather jacket. He barely knew the guy except that he was a senior. "Lucky dude," Henry said to himself. Then he saw another guy with the same jacket. Then a girl walked by, and *she* was wearing one. Before he had taken his seat in English class, he had seen two more students wearing fringe suede leather jackets. And there was another one in that first period class. They were all sweating like crazy and looking at each other in disbelief. Henry's jacket generated some comments, one senior boy telling Henry he looked like an outlaw biker and another suggesting he cut the sleeves off and make it a vest.

Second period was biology and Henry was already seated when Joyce walked in. The class was arranged with double desks. She sat right down where Henry was situated and said, "I like your jacket!" That was a thrill — but it lasted only a couple of minutes because this other girl, Helena, who was friendly with Joyce, asked him to move so she could sit there. Joyce just smiled wanly at Henry and nodded, so he took another seat nearby. Maybe it was for the better, he thought. Anyway, during the period, Joyce turned and smiled warmly at him several times and they walked together to their side-by-side lockers.

"I hope you don't mind moving over to let Helena sit there," Joyce said. "She takes really good notes."

"That's okay." Then, to change the subject, he said, "Hey, did you see all the kids wearing fringed suede leather jackets?"

"Yeah. Most of them are taking them off and hanging them in their lockers. I guess it's the heat."

"I'm thinking they're embarrassed. They probably begged their parents for the money and figured they'd be, like, exclusive. There must be forty kids who have them. The latest rage, I guess."

"But you're the only one I've seen with a Levi's jacket. I think that's much better. If they become the latest rage, you'll be at the start instead of the middle."

Henry never saw a single one of those fringe suede leather jackets again at school and he learned to bless the penury of his mom and dad, and not for the last time. Joyce's approval meant a lot to him. It gave him confidence, and confidence is what is always needed when a kid starts dreaming romantic dreams.

Three Poems
by Joel Wilson

"The Cherry Picker"

A dozen men, or likes of them
Under tree and sun;
Damning God for bearing fruit. All toil in crew, save one.
A dime a bushel, five will do—
The payman comes at noon.
A crooked back and a broken soul
Get drunk, and then move on.

"The Siege"

Under fire
No-name bodies
Huddle like fading coals.
Blood runs fast and slow and stops
And pounds the ears with fear.
Hunger wastes, wounds, kills—
Only the rats are victors.
Flashing steel and lead
Make puddles out of men,
And children burn and stink;
All to change a flag.

"Dear John"

I had lunch with your mother today.
The weather is warm and sunny.
I'm getting a job this vacation.
Just think of all that money!
School is okay, I guess,
But you know how things are.
Too bad you cannot be here.
That place somehow seems so far.
My Daddy just bought a new Ford.
Your guess what he needs one for.
You know he has two already.
P.S. I love you no more.

Authors' Biographies

Bruce is blessed to be a son and a father, happily a brother, honored to be a veteran, lucky to be an author (*Death in the Black Patch*, © 2016, *No Place That Far*, © 2020, and *Muckrakers 1917,* available June 2025), a professor, above all else, eternally happy to be a husband.

Chas retired as a Lieutenant Colonel after 24 years of service in the United States Army. He followed that with 22 years as a Financial Advisor. He is now fully retired and lives in Meridian, Idaho, where he is working on his first novel.

Howard is 71 years old, and like his character Henry, has been an advocate of Romance his entire life and has met with success in this ambition as demonstrated by a 48-year marriage to his lovely wife Leslie. As a writer, he is an award-winning poet, receiving $25.00 for a villanelle he composed at Fullerton (CA) Junior College in 1973. In the mid-1980's, he wrote a series of articles for Baseball Hobby News and has turned to short fiction in his semi-retirement. He now lives in Fullerton with his lovely wife Leslie.